OPEN DOORS

K. C. KNIGHT

ACT ONE PUBLISHING

Act One Publishing

For information on upcoming novels for Knight Books please visit our website at www.kristinaclaireknight.com

Cover Illustrated by Miguel Montejano

First edition manufactured in Houston, Texas, United States of America.

Library of Congress Control Number
2 0 2 0 9 1 7 9 4 1

ISBN 978-1-7356736-0-8 (Paperback)
ISBN 978-1-7356736-2-2 (Hardback)
ISBN 978-1-7356736-1-5 (Ebook)

This book is dedicated to Ashley, Alex, and Casey.
You are my inspiration.

CONTENTS

INTO THE BAYOU

*I*t was a cool October night when Charlotte set out
for her evening routine before turning into bed. Her
dark brown hair hung slightly below her shoulders and
although she was well into her seventies, everyone told her she
didn't look a day over sixty. She had always done everything she
could to hold back Father Time, including an ongoing war she
had with some invading grey streaks. She battled them relentlessly with several boxes of store-bought dye, determined to be
the victor. She had deep green eyes and was a well-dressed and
well-liked woman in the small town of St. Francisville. Her
white two-story house was set on a plantation back in the bayou
of Louisiana, with vines that seemed to grow out of the roof
itself and hang down around the sides of the house. Huge
willow trees swept through her front yard and the bayou
surrounded her on the empty hilltop. Charlotte's home was well
kept with everything in its place, much like an old antique shop,
with lots of trinkets from years past. All of her memories now
sat upon the shelves in the form of shot glasses, pictures, and
knickknacks from around the world.

Pouring herself a glass of wine, she hoped it would help her sleep a little better through the night. Lately, the dark in the quiet house had been keeping her up and disturbing her sleep. The wooden floors creaked as she walked into her bedroom and opened the window to let in the fresh air. She loved the feel of the cold wind blowing in and the smell of the flowers and trees as they fought their way through the bayou at night. The sound of the crickets and frogs played almost like a nightly symphony that would somehow make her feel a little less alone in that big empty house. As she shut her bedroom door, she reached up and bolted a lock at the top of the door. She had called a lock-smith about a month ago and had the lock installed. There were things she had seen in the house that she would tell no one about.

Climbing into bed, she took a sip of her wine, and grabbed her favorite book from the nightstand. Reading often helped her fall asleep, and she liked to read the words aloud to give the story more theatrics, almost like she was in the book herself. She began to read.

'Be mindful of the darkness, watchful of the evil around you. For he will send his demons to torment you and pull you in. Their evil goes un-noticed, hiding in the shadows, they will haunt your mind at night. They are the whispers in the dark, pulling you into self-destruction. They are the...'

Through the quiet came a loud sound from the bathroom next to her room. With a quick breath, she jerked her head up and turned her eyes towards the room, listening intently.

Tap. Tap. Tap. The echoing sound filled the bathroom like the tip of a fingernail hitting hard against the marble countertop three times, and Charlotte froze. The door was open, and in the dim light she could see nothing was there. Her eyes fixated on the empty room, and when silence finally won over time, she thought it to be nothing more than her imagination or maybe the effects of the wine. She settled back down, regaining her position in the warm bed and continued to read.

'He is the demon that will come through any open door. You must be...'

Tap. Tap. Tap. She jerked her head up again, as her eyes darted quickly towards the sound that had returned.

"Stop it!" she yelled. "Leave me alone!" A tightness filled her chest as she struggled to keep her thoughts from scattering. Reaching for the glass on the nightstand, she finished her wine with one quick gulp.

The night was quiet, and once again the tapping had stopped. She closed her book and reached for the remote. She hoped the television would take her mind off the haunting sounds that were still stalking her thoughts. She laid in bed, mindlessly staring at the television as she slowly drifted off into a deep sleep.

The wind blew and the chimes on the front porch clinked together like tiny bells as the wooden swing creaked back and forth. The hours passed through the night, until the chimes were the only sounds you could hear drifting through the old house. Charlotte's television had gone silent, and a slideshow of pictures played in a loop. Moving through the house, a dark shadow appeared, and a cold breeze swept over Charlotte's body as she slept. In the darkness, the faceless figure stopped at the foot of her bed. Fixating its glare upon her, it moved slowly to her side, reaching for her ankle, running the tips of its long fingers softly up her leg and across her fragile skin. Tilting back its head, its mouth dropped open and whispers flooded out into the air. Charlotte became restless, twitching in her sleep and began to dream.

SHE COULD STILL FEEL *the warmth of her bed and the soft pillow beneath her head. Glancing around her room, she felt a bit in a daze. Red wine moved slightly in the bottom of her wine glass, as if she had just placed it on the table. Her blue robe draped over the* old yellow chair in the corner of the room. She looked at the television playing its usual selection of ocean pictures, as it often did late into the night. A slight chill filled the air as the wind blew through the curtains. Her mind awoke as she pointlessly struggled to move.

Lying on her bed, she began to tremble as fear overtook her, and an evil essence filled the room. A light pierced through the window and cascaded off her fragile legs. A dark shadowy figure lingered at the foot of her bed, its deep red eyes glaring, as if it were looking right through her. It seemed to steal the very breath she gasped for. She stiffened as a chill shot through her veins. Blackness filled the inside of her and a pressure pounded through her head like a loud echo in a deep abandoned cave. Her skin froze beneath the touch of its wretched hands as it grasped her legs and climbed onto her body. She began to shiver as the creature's unbearable weight pinned her completely. Her eyes were glued open, too afraid to blink. Her voice struggled to scream, but only silence filled the air. The creature stared down at her, and a deep voice quietly whispered, "Nothing can help you this time." She fought to catch her breath, but the air felt shallow as it desperately tried to make its way to her lungs. Her brittle bones began to give way as the pressure upon her chest grew heavier. The beast's fingers pressed into the pulse of her throat. The touch of its hand on her skin felt cold, as it wrapped its long fingers around her neck and began to squeeze. Her throat began to close up as the grip became tighter and tighter. Gasping for air, her eyes fixated upon the eyes of the shadow engulfing her. She felt a sharp piercing of its nails as they cut deep into her skin, and something cold and wet began to slowly run down her neck. The terrifying thought repeatedly played in her mind: 'I'll never breathe again.' Charlotte could hear the sound of her heart beating louder and louder until it drowned out the silence of the night, and slowly everything faded to black.

. . .

A LOUD GASP for air filled the room, as the dark shadow moved back through the house. Charlotte's lifeless body lay across her bed, her eyes wide open, her weathered face still wearing a look of terror, as a drop of blood dripped slowly from her lips. A door upstairs creaked as it closed and the house returned to silence.

INTO THE GROUND

*E*arly Friday morning, the sound of a phone ringing filled the small two-bedroom townhouse of Jason and Claire Cole. Jason nearly tripped over a ball rolling down the hall across the wooden floor. Straightening his tie for work, he reached to grab the call.

"Hello," he pulled the phone away from his mouth just long enough to yell down the hall, "Sara, get your ball before it kills me!"

Sara ran through the apartment, but the sound of her laughing was quickly drowned out by the voice on the other end of the line. "Mr. Cole? I've been trying to reach you. Your grandmother... she was found dead a few nights ago." The sentence hung in the air like a thick fog. As the caller's voice drifted off into a series of pointless details, Jason could hear nothing but those few words.

The news of Charlotte's death came unexpectedly. Jason slumped down into the chair, next to the table, his eyes filled with tears. He tried to steady his voice as it trembled. "Thank you for calling. Yes, I understand. I'll be there in the morning."

Claire walked into the room picking up the toys as Jason sat quietly staring into space.

"Sara, get your backpack for school." Claire raised her eyebrows, tilting her head to the side to look closer at Jason. "What's wrong? What happened?"

Jason wiped his eyes and gazed up at her as if he had just lost his best friend. "It's my grandmother," he paused. "She... passed away."

Claire leaned silently against the doorframe, then sat next to Jason. "I... What? Oh Jason." She pulled him close to her as tears ran down her face. "I'm so sorry." In a lot of ways, Charlotte had been like a mother to Claire. Claire's own mother had died when she was very young, and Charlotte lived a few houses down the street. After Claire's mother passed away, Charlotte would bring food to her house and check on her almost every day. Claire struggled to keep her composure. "What happened?"

Jason shrugged, staring down at his hands. "She died in her sleep." He found a bit of comfort in knowing she had passed peacefully. "Claire, are you okay?" He pushed her hair away from her face and wiped her tears from her cheek. They both practically grew up at Charlotte's house, and he knew it was just as difficult for her to process this as it was for him.

It had been a while since they had visited his grandmother and the small town. Shifting in the chair, Claire took a deep breath and reached for Jason's hand. "I know how you feel about going back to that town. Is there anything I can do?"

Running his fingers through his thick hair, and shaking his head back and forth, he pulled himself up, still in disbelief. "It's okay, the accident was a long time ago. By now I'm sure it's not making the daily headlines." He wiped the tears off his cheek; he always shoved every emotion deep down when he was nervous or upset. "I've needed to face going back for a long time. I'll go in the morning and sort out the details, and make the necessary arrangements." Turning away from Claire, he rubbed his eyes and grabbed his jacket. "I need to get to work. I have a class in thirty minutes." He pulled Claire close to him and hugged her tightly. "Are you sure you're okay?" Claire nodded her head, but was clearly not okay. "You better get Sara to school, you don't want her to miss her party today." He kissed her softly and left for work.

Just then Sara came running around the corner. "I'm a princess today!"

"Yes, you are," Claire said, clearing her throat and bending down to give Sara a hug, "We better get going." She loaded Sara into her car and took a deep breath before pulling out of the driveway. Sara had a kindergarten party today for Halloween, and Claire had volunteered to take pictures for the school. She had developed into a successful photographer, and had earned the reputation of being one of the best in Houston. She drove to the school, as if on autopilot, with her memories of Charlotte fighting to drown out the sound of Sara singing 'Let It Go' from the back seat, until finally the past was victorious, and the singing became nothing more than a muffled background noise. It had been years since she had seen Charlotte. Only once at Christmas, when Sara was still a baby, had they gone for a visit. Time seemed to pass so quickly these days. With her studio and Jason teaching at the high school, there always seem to be something that came up. Now more than anything she wished she would have made more time to visit Charlotte. She would miss the stories Charlotte would tell, while they sat on the front porch swing, sipping wine. She would miss Charlotte.

As Jason drove to work, his mind began to wander, thinking about his childhood and growing up in St. Francisville. He rubbed the back of his neck, and blew out a series of short breaths, as he tried to control the thoughts of returning to the small town. He had worked through a lot of issues since they moved away, but the questions surrounding his mother's death were always with him.

It was the mid-Eighties when his mother Cindy and he had first moved to Louisiana to be closer to her mother. Cindy had to work long hours to make ends meet after her divorce, and having Charlotte close by was a huge help. Unfortunately, Jason's father had more important things to do than sticking around to help raise a kid or to pay child support. After all, he won the ticket in the divorce for a fresh start at being single, and he was more than happy to take it. The last Jason heard from him, he was slipping off into another bottle of whiskey, somewhere in another dive bar. After a short time, he stopped calling altogether and replaced Jason and Cindy with a more suitable dysfunctional family. It was everything Cindy could do to work and keep food on the table. Jason was all she cared about, and the thought of failing him was never an option.

Charlotte loved having her daughter and grandson around and truth be told, Jason was the center of her world. He loved everything about growing up in the bayou. After school, he jumped on his bike and headed straight for her house. The smell of the fresh country air and the feel of the dirt road bouncing beneath his tires, made him feel like he was on an adventure every day. Freshly baked cookies filled his grandmother's house daily and he wasn't the only one that looked forward to them. That's where he first met Claire, the girl with dark hair and big blue eyes. She stole his heart from the moment they met. She was always at Charlotte's house, taking pictures of everything. Claire's mom had left her a set of cameras when she passed away. She always had one in her hand, as if it were a security blanket she couldn't live without. Charlotte was a great story-teller. She had the two of them laughing so hard they would forget their problems. Those summers were the best part of Jason's childhood: swimming in the pool in the backyard, sitting on the pier, fishing in the pond, and playing board games with Charlotte and Claire. Listening to Charlotte's tales of the mysterious witch that haunted the swamps in the bayou looking for her lost child. The story gave Jason and Claire the chills, but they loved how Charlotte told it.

They soon became close friends, and everywhere Jason went, Claire wasn't far behind. If there was such a thing as soul mates, then they were the definition. It was no surprise to anyone when they married, shortly after college, before moving away.

It was hard to believe that was so long ago, and memories of those days felt almost like a different life. They were in their mid-thirties now, and Jason's once wavy, dirty blonde hair had been replaced by a much shorter haircut, worthy of society. The days of running barefoot in the bayou had been traded in for a pair of dress shoes and a concrete road to success. His fishing pole that once stayed glued in his hand was now nothing more than a black briefcase.

Jason sat in his truck in the parking lot of the school, and images of the bayou flooded his thoughts. He felt a churning in the bottom of his stomach as he fumbled with the door handle repeatedly as if he were in a trance. Visions of his mother's unexplained car accident flashed through his mind. Her death came just a couple of months before Jason and Claire finished college and it was the talk of the town for quite some time. Jason's hands began to sweat as he wiped them on his trousers and took a deep breath, He glanced at his reflection in the rearview mirror. The thought of returning to the town filled him with angst. They moved long ago, to leave it all behind, but now he would have to go back. He owed it to Charlotte. He walked in the school, numb to everything around him. On zombie mode he struggled his way through his classes and the day's monotonous routine.

* * *

CLAIRE REACHED THE SCHOOL, unpacking her equipment as Sara climbed out of the backseat of the car and rushed towards the school doors. "Not so fast, Sara," she called out. Struggling with her light stands, she tried to keep up with the excited little princess. As they went through the doors, ghosts, pirates and witches filled the school hallways. "Sara, slow down," Claire called out, but Sara was on hyper-speed today, rushing into her classroom. After all, it was Halloween.

After lunch, little princesses and superheroes all lined up to take their special picture. As each child moved through the line, smiling and making silly faces, one by one the flashes overtook Claire's thoughts. Once again, her mind drifted into the past, into the bayou, sitting on the front porch, listening to Charlotte. She couldn't believe she was gone. Pain filled her chest and she hid her face as she wiped the tears from her eyes. It was everything she could do to wear a fake smile and make it through the day. When the last bell finally rang and school was over, no one was more relieved than Claire.

FINALLY HOME, Jason collapsed on the bed, after a long day of nothingness. He closed his eyes, and quickly fell asleep. When Claire returned home, she walked in and covered Jason with a blanket before returning to the living room with Sara. The day continued and the next thing Jason knew, the alarm clock was sounding, and it was time to get up and face his fears.

On Saturday morning, Jason packed his bags and set out towards St. Francisville. He had a meeting with a lawyer in town, Fred Williams, who was handling Charlotte's estate. As he drove the long stretch of 1-10 that ran from Houston to Louisiana, he tried to take deep breaths and think of the happier times in the small town, but flashes of the accident kept fighting their way into his thoughts. The closer he got, the more Jason's stomach began to twist into knots. As he reached St Francisville and pulled into the parking lot at the end of Main Street, he took a deep breath and glanced in the mirror before getting out of the truck. He couldn't help but notice how time had stood still in the small town. The streets were lined with old red brick buildings and painted shops, straight out of an old movie. Walking down the road, he glanced around and it seemed to get a little easier to breathe again. The place had the old-fashioned charm of a Norman Rockwell painting, and the smell of clean country air. He noticed the bookstore, the general store and even the ice cream parlor were exactly as he had remembered. Jason stopped for a moment and looked up and down the street where he grew up. He looked at the old bank his mother used to take him to every Friday to deposit her check, and the church on the hill with the big willow tree hanging down in front. Charlotte and Cindy took him there every Sunday morning, where he would nervously sit next to Claire. He looked at the stores and remembered the times he and his mom would come to Main Street, singing silly made-up songs as they walked down the sidewalks past the little shops. He missed his mom greatly and now he would miss Charlotte as well. He loved the days they would go for ice cream or stop at the bookstore to grab a book. For the first time since the accident, Jason found comfort in the small town and in the memories of his child-hood. For a moment, just a moment, he felt a slight peace with the past.

"Jason Cole?" an older man wearing a plaid shirt stepped out from a nearby office and turned towards Jason.

"Yes," Jason replied, glancing at the man as he pulled his mind out of the past and back to reality.

"I'm Fred Williams, I thought that might be you. We don't get a lot of visitors," he laughed as he reached to shake Jason's hand. "You want to step into my office?"

"Yes, thank you, it's nice to meet you," Jason replied, shaking his hand and taking one final glance back up the street into his past. He followed Fred Williams up a flight of stairs and into an office with a big brown desk covered with stacks of papers and two yellow chairs. Jason looked around the room and back at Fred, he couldn't help but think to himself how much everything looked like a scene straight out of a bad porno movie from the Seventies, with the fat, hairy guy as the star.

Mr. Williams handed Jason a stack of papers. "Have a seat. I'm sorry for your loss, you have my deepest condolences. Your grandmother was a wonderful woman. I knew her personally. She made all of her arrangements ahead of time for the funeral. She didn't want anyone to be bothered. That's just how she was. All you have to do is select the date and she has everything else settled. I have the keys to her house and well…" The heavy-set man settled back in his chair, clearing his throat. "She left everything to you."

"That's what it's come down to," Jason thought. "My grandmother's entire life now clipped into a stack of papers on a clipboard, in an old porno movie." The only thing needed now was for a scantily clad secretary to enter the room and plop up on the desk with her tits out. Jason pulled his thoughts together.

Reading over everything, he took a deep breath and signed the papers. "Who found her?" he asked.

"Oh, a friend of hers that owns the bookstore down the street, her name is Kristina Graves. I guess she was visiting and found it strange when she didn't answer the door. Used the spare key and found her lying on the bed." He took back the signed documents from Jason and put them into a file, behind his desk. "It's a damn shame. Anything you folks need, just let me know."

"Thank you for everything," Jason said, shaking Fred's hand. He headed out of the office, walking slowly back down the street towards the parking lot.

"It's done," he thought, as he climbed into the front seat of his truck and closed the door.

He drove down the dirt road, back into the bayou towards the old plantation home that once belonged to his grandmother and now belonged to him. As Jason reached the bridge where the accident happened, he felt a sickening ache in the bottom of his stomach, and he pulled the truck to a stop. He rolled the window down and staring out at the old wooden bridge, he took a deep breath and tried to push the memory from his mind. Slowly he began to drive the truck across the bridge. In the faint distance, he thought he could hear his mother screaming his name. Trying to ignore the sound, he wiped the sweat from his brow and stopped the truck. His vision became blurred, and the pounding in his head grew louder and louder.

He remembered the last time he saw his mom, standing in the living room of their small apartment. Her smile was contagious, her laugh... he missed her deeply. No matter how many years passed, there was nothing that would fill the hole of her being gone or the guilt he felt of not going with her that fatal night. "If I would have just went, maybe, none of this would have happened." Visions of the car flipping off the side of the bridge and plunging into the water beneath filled his mind. The claw marks on top of the car... the claw marks... the pounding in his head had now progressed to a painful throbbing, and he could barely catch his breath. Too many unanswered questions surrounded the accident, leaving him empty inside. Gasping a deep breath, he slowly backed the truck up and the bridge in front of him held tightly onto the past. He decided to take another road and go the long way around to get to the house. He couldn't bring himself to cross the bridge and the farther he was from it, the better he began to feel.

Pulling up the driveway, he let out a sigh of relief, he found comfort being at the house, he felt.... safe. All of the time he had played there as a boy fought its way to the front of his memories. Even though the house looked like it needed a bit of fixing up and a fresh coat of paint, it still held the charm of the old plantation home he remembered. Looking back on the memories he had in the town with Charlotte and his mom; it was hard to believe they were both gone. "Sometimes you have to face your fears to try and move past them," he thought. A phrase that stuck with him from months of therapy. Something about being at the house made him feel a little closer to both of them. As he stepped out of his truck, he sucked the smell of the country air in and the thoughts of the wooden bridge faded. For a second, he thought he could actually smell his grandmother's freshly baked cookies. Everything in that moment, from the wind blowing past him, to the rocky dirt crumbling beneath his boots, was calling him back to the small town. His thoughts filled with flashes of Sara running through the fields laughing, just as he and Claire had done so many years before. The wind started to pick up, and a huge gust blew through the trees. A strange sense overtook him. The accident was hiding far from his mind, and in that moment, Jason knew what he wanted to do. The clouds shifted in the sky above him, and as he took out his phone and called Claire, a black crow landed on the front porch and caught his eye.

Claire answered quickly, and was surprised at the enthusiasm in Jason's voice.

"Claire, how would you feel about moving back? At least for a while until I can sort all of this out. It's weird being here after all this time but everything is so... quiet and I think it might be good for Sara."

Claire paused for a few seconds. "Jason, are you sure? You know I have always wanted to go back but... How are you? I, I miss you."

Jason started to walk around the side of the house, still turning back a bit to lock eyes with the crow perched on the railing. "I'm okay. It's strange being back after all this time but at the same time... it feels like home." He looked into the backyard at the once blue swimming pool that had now turned a deep mossy green. "It's definitely going to take some work to clean this place up but I think my grandmother would have wanted us here, after all, she left it to us, and we're the only ones left to take care of it. Even if we decide to sell, it will take months to get this place ready."

Smiling, Claire let out a sigh of relief. It had taken Jason quite some time and a lot of therapy to move past the guilt he felt about Cindy's death, and she wasn't sure how he would handle Charlotte's. She was relieved. Deep down, she thought it might help him finally have some closure. "Alright, whatever you want to do, I'm with you." She hung up the phone and glanced around the townhouse. In the pit of her stomach she could feel it: everything was about to change, and as much as she had always wanted to go home, there was something about change that always made her nervous.

Jason unlocked the back door and stepped inside the house. Charlotte's house was always clean with everything in its place. It was as if nothing had changed from the last time he was there, but this time the house was full of silence, as if it were asleep. A dim light showed through the curtains and hit the walls as he walked through the house. Overwhelmed with emotion, it hit him. There would be no more laughter, and no more stories from Charlotte. Jason wiped the tears from his eyes, as he sat down at the table in the kitchen. A door shut softly upstairs and Jason jerked his head up and looked towards the stairs. His very presence seemed to have awakened something in the house and Jason got up and moved towards the staircase. "Hello?" Looking up at the top of the stairs, he began repeating a rhythmic chant to himself, "Face your fears, face your fears," as he walked slowly up the stairs. "Anyone here?" he called out. The wooden steps creaked beneath his boots as he reached the top of the stairs and glanced around the empty game room. He could barely see the old pool table sitting in the middle of the room collecting dust.

He opened the door to the bathroom at the top of the stairs, flipped on the light and took a quick glance back around the game room but nothing was there. The blue shower curtain with purple and black dragonflies was pulled closed in the bathroom and Jason moved slowly towards it. Charlotte had a thing for dragonflies and they were a running theme throughout the house. He jerked back the curtain and rolling his eyes he let out a slight chuckle and a sigh of relief. Nothing... "This whole thing is starting to get to me," he thought, and he left the room and started back down the stairs. Stopping halfway down, he turned around and walked back upstairs and opened the door to the bedroom, next to the bathroom. He used to stay in that room when he was younger and visited Charlotte. The bed still sat in the corner of the room next to the window that looked out into the front yard and he walked over and pulled back the curtain. It was a beautiful sight to see after so long. Being back in the town after his mothers' accident would still be an adjustment, but one he was finally willing to face. The small town offered something that you couldn't get living in the big city. Filet mignon was great but sometimes all you needed was a good old burger. He wanted to give Sara the same chance to grow up here, where he and Claire had. The same opportunity to slow down and feel the pace of life, instead of running through the hours like a marathon. Now there would be nothing more to do but say goodbye to Charlotte. Jason closed the curtain and walked back down the stairs.

* * *

CHARLOTTE WAS ALWAYS one to try and save money and in her last wish, she did just that. She had set up a graveside service, skipping all the formalities of a viewing and traditional funeral. The service would be short and sweet and held at St. Francisville's Sandlot Cemetery. Jason set it up for the following

Saturday to allow Claire and Sara time to settle things at home and make it to Louisiana.

He stayed in the house, for what seemed like the longest week, waiting for them to arrive. The sound of Claire's car pulling up the driveway was the best thing Jason had heard in days. He walked outside and stopped on the porch to look at Claire as she got out of the car. She brushed her hair out of her face as it blew in the breeze, and Jason thought she looked twenty-two again. She had always been a beautiful woman, but something about that moment made Jason take a deep breath. It was easy to see, standing in the backdrop of the plantation, that Claire belonged there. She was like a missing piece of a puzzle that just fell into place. He walked over and hugged her tightly, "I'm so glad you're here."

"Me too," Claire said, looking up at the old house as Sara climbed out of the back seat. "Daddy! Daddy!" Sara ran over and jumped into Jason's arms. "Is this our new house?"

"It sure is," Jason glanced back at Claire. "Come on." He carried Sara in the house and she squirmed out of his arms as soon as they stepped inside. She darted from room to room discovering their new home as if it were a candy store she had stepped into for the first time.

"Which room is mine?" she asked, looking at Claire with a wide grin and jumping up and down. Her long blonde hair bounced off her shoulders as she pulled on Claire's arm.

Jason looked back at her and laughed at her excitement. "Top of the stairs. I always stayed in that room when I visited here growing up and now it's yours."

"Woo hoo!" Sara exclaimed, as she took off running up the stairs to explore her new bedroom. As she reached the top of the stairs, she let out another scream of excitement, "Pool ball!" Jason and Claire looked at each other and laughed.

* * *

THE NEXT MORNING was a beautiful one, as Claire and Jason dressed to prepare themselves for Charlotte's funeral. The drive to the cemetery was quiet, while memories of Charlotte went through both of their minds. As they arrived, they were surprised to see so many people had turned out for the grave-side service. They sat quietly under the green tent which covered the ground where Charlotte would be laid to rest. The pastor read from scriptures, and they sang Amazing Grace, then the service came to a close. Jason couldn't help but notice a slender black woman wearing a flowing black dress, standing off in the distance, watching the funeral. Everyone began to form the uncomfortable line that passes the family at funerals. People they recognized and some they didn't would come through and offer their condolences. Jason shook hands and looked past them as he watched the woman get into her car and drive away. Finally, everyone left, and they were the last ones standing by Charlotte's casket.

Jason laid a red rose on top of the casket, holding on to Claire's hand tightly and giving it a slight squeeze. "Goodbye grandma, I love you."

"Goodbye Charlotte, we will miss you so much," Claire said, looking down and wiping the tears from her face, as she placed a white rose next to Jason's. A dragonfly landed on the casket for a brief moment and then flew away. Claire looked at Jason, but they said nothing of the coincidence. He grabbed Sara's hand and they walked back to the car.

Two men took down the tent, put away the chairs and prepared to lower Charlotte's casket into the ground. As Claire and Jason drove away, the casket dropped further and further, deep down into the dark hole. Inside the ground, hands bloated with rot, pushed their way through the dirt, grabbing the casket on both sides, aiding Charlotte's descent to the bottom of the grave. The flowers once elegantly placed atop the casket were now muffled under scoops of earth shoveled from above.

THE SHADOW

*S*everal months had gone by since Charlotte passed away and they moved into the old house. The summer months were here and the searing heat blanketed the bayou like a sand sheet in the desert. Sun tea jars filled the front porches as it took gallons of sweet tea to make it through the smoldering months. Jason had started teaching at the local high school, and though Claire was finding it more difficult than anticipated to build clientele in a small town, she was quickly becoming the town's go-to photographer for every community event.

The house was much bigger than their townhouse and took some getting used to for all of them. Jason and Claire's room was downstairs off the main living room; it was Charlotte's old room. It made Claire nervous to have Sara sleep so far away from her and so close to the stairs. The three bedrooms upstairs hadn't had guests in years; however, the beds were neatly made and pictures of dragonflies hung in each of the rooms. The second story was like a giant playroom that kept Sara busy most of the day. The attic was over Jason and Claire's room, which had an entry door off of the game room. It was the only room they had yet to clean out. The swimming pool had finally been restored to its once-beautiful shade of blue, and a pond filled with fish was just beyond the field. Jason looked forward to taking Sara fishing in the days to come. He had spent hours on that pier as a boy, and his fishing poles and tackle were most likely still in the old shed, untouched by time. The yard seemed endless, and the willow trees hung low everywhere you looked. Charlotte had a green thumb, and it showed in every part of her landscaped grounds.

* * *

"Sara!" Claire yelled, casting a glance towards the stairs. "Come downstairs and get your toys!"

Claire was cleaning up around the house and preparing dinner.

"Sara, come down!" she called again, putting the blanket down and gripping the handrail at the bottom of the stairs. She paused for a moment before walking back towards the kitchen.

Smoke was coming out of a pot on the stove and the smell of beef stew filled the air as she picked up a large spoon and began to stir.

A dark shadow drifted slowly across the game room, and Sara froze as it caught her eye.

Frustrated, Claire yelled out again, looking back towards the staircase, "Sara!"

Sara's heart began to beat faster and her body felt glued to the floor as she clinched her doll tightly and fixated upon the shadow. It stopped and hovered in the corner of the room, turning back as if Sara had caught its attention as well.

Claire slammed the spoon down on the counter. "Sara!" She turned and quickly began to walk up the stairs. "Come on, I know you can hear me!"

Sara could barely hear anything over the fear that was taking on a deafening silence inside of her head, as she watched the shadow slowly disappear from sight.

Claire stopped at the top of the stairs as she stood in the bedroom doorway. "What are you doing?" She could see the scared look on Sara's face and her tone immediately changed. "What is it?" She glanced back into the game room where Sara was staring intensely, then focused back on Sara.

Sara sat still and was unable to force any words from her mouth as she stared into the room.

Claire turned and looked again, taking more time to evaluate every corner of the room as she walked around the pool table. She noticed the attic door was slightly open, and thought Sara's actions to be nothing more than a hand caught in the cookie jar. She had been told to stay away from the attic until it could be cleaned out.

"Sara! I told you to stay out of there, you could get hurt!" Claire slammed the attic door. "Come on!" She reached down and grabbed Sara's hand pulling her up to her feet.

Sara got up quickly and went with Claire, back downstairs never saying a word about the shadow.

"Pick up your toys and put them in your room before your dad gets home."

Sara reluctantly began to pick up her toys as she kept her eyes glued to the top of the stairs. Slowly, taking one step at a time, she moved closer to the game room. Her eyes widened as she reached her bedroom, throwing her toys in a pile, before running back down the stairs.

When Jason came in the door, they sat down to eat dinner. Sara's stomach felt sick, and she quietly picked at her food, looking down at her plate, not saying a word.

Jason searched Claire and Sara's faces as he tried to figure out the awkward silence in the room. "Everything go okay today?" he asked.

"Sara's just getting into things she shouldn't," Claire said, shaking her head and giving Sara a side glance.

Sara shifted in her seat and stared up at Claire. Her voice took on a slight tremble. "But I didn't..."

Claire's voice softened as she reached over and rubbed Sara's arm. "It's okay, just stay out of there, you could get hurt."

"What am I missing?" Jason asked.

"Sara was messing around in the attic," Claire answered, as she got up and started to clear the plates from the table.

Sara rolled her eyes and dropped her spoon on her plate. "But I..."

"Sara, please stay out of there, and away from the pool," Jason interrupted, pointing his finger at her.

Sara sighed, looking down at her plate. She pushed it away from her, and crossed her arms.

"Well, if you're finished," Claire reached over and took Sara's plate, ignoring her behavior, so as not to add to the situation, "then it's time for your bath. Go up and I'll be there in a minute to tuck you in bed."

Sara shoved her chair away from the table and stomped up the stairs. She paused for a quick second when she reached the top, surveyed the game room and ran into her room to grab her pajamas. Jason picked up his plate and put it in the sink. "You know, her teenage years are going to be great." He smiled at Claire, which made her laugh a little.

Claire leaned over and kissed him. "I'll go help her. Thank God she is only five!" she laughed, "we have a long way to go before those years, and then you can handle her." She walked up the stairs and put on her mommy smile.

Sara was still sitting in the bathtub when Claire reached the bathroom. "Hey, come on. Let's get you out of there and tucked into bed." She reached over and lifted Sara out of the bathtub. Grabbing a towel, she began to dry Sara's hair and get her dressed for bed.

"Mommy, I didn't open the attic door. I promise," Sara pleaded, as she attempted one last time to prove her case, before giving up completely on her innocence.

Claire bent down, picking Sara up. She carried her into the room and laid her on the bed. She sat down next to her, brushing her hair out of her face. "Sara, the attic can be dangerous. Daddy and I haven't had a chance to clean it out yet and there are a bunch of boxes and stuff stored in there. I just don't want you to get hurt." She kissed her on the forehead and turned the closet light on as she started to walk out of the room. "Do you want me to leave your door open?"

The closet light scattered across Sara's pale face as she jerked herself straight up and grabbed her doll, "No!"

Claire raised her eyebrows and looked back at Sara. "Okay, I'll close it."

"Mommy, I'm scared," Sara said, still sitting straight up.

"It's okay, there is nothing to be scared of." Walking back towards the bed, Claire reached up and grabbed a beautiful glass dragonfly off the shelf. She sat on the edge of the bed and showed it to Sara. "You know, dragonflies were once said to have magical powers."

"They were?" Sara asked, as she rubbed her eyes and lay back down.

"They belonged to the fairies from another world that lived deep underground in a special cave. It was said the fairies would travel from their world to ours and protect all the children from the shadow world that lay beyond. One day the fairies had a great danger approach them and they cast a special spell on the dragonflies giving them the power to protect children, and they released them into our world forever. That's why Great Grandma filled the house with them. She used to tell your dad and me that story all the time." She sat the dragonfly on the nightstand next to Sara's bed. "This one will watch over you and keep you safe." She leaned down and kissed Sara on the head. "Goodnight princess."

As Claire began to walk out of the room, Sara reached up, grabbing the dragonfly close to her and rolled over in bed. "Goodnight Mommy. I love you."

"I love you too." She shut the door and walked back downstairs shaking her head back and forth as she went into their bedroom. She crawled into bed next to Jason, rolling over and laying her head upon his chest.

"I told Sara the dragonfly story," Claire said, looking up at Jason. "Do you remember that?"

"Oh yeah," Jason said. "I think I slept with that dragonfly every night when I was here as a kid." He laughed. "It's funny the things you believe as a child."

Claire stared up at the bedroom door. "Why do you think there is a dead bolt on the door?" she asked.

"I don't know." He rolled over to hold her. "My grandmother had it put on a while back."

"You don't think it's odd?" she asked, glancing back at Jason.

"I think my grandmother was a little odd," he laughed, pulling Claire closer to him.

"You're funny." Smiling, she snuggled up to him and pulled the covers over them tightly as if to cocoon them for the night.

The house was dark and quiet. The wind blew outside, and the sound of the wind chimes clinking on the front porch filled the night air. Upstairs in the game room, the attic door creaked slowly open, and Sara began to toss and turn in her bed. The more the door opened the more restless she became. Piercing through the night, a black shadowy figure stopped just outside of Sara's door. It stood still for a few minutes, lingering as if it could see through the door. Finally, it turned and continued slowly down the stairs. As it descended down the stairwell, Sara returned to a peaceful sleep.

The dark figure crept into Jason and Claire's room. It stood still at the foot of their bed, watching them sleep like a predator picking out its next prey. Its long fingers slid across the footrail as it started to move closer to Jason. Clearly, he had been chosen as the next meal. While the dark figure hovered closely above Jason's body, almost touching his skin, its mouth dropped wide open and it let out an eerie whisper. Jason became restless, tossing and turning, muttering under his breath as he began to dream.

WALKING BEHIND THE HOUSE, he felt pulled towards the field. The wind tousled his hair and a breeze shot across his face like ice. The wet grass flattened beneath his feet as the cold blades swept across his ankles. The crickets and frogs took over the bayou, drowning out the silence of the foggy night. In the distance, a ruffling of sticks broke beneath heavy footsteps. He reached the edge of the field, pushing the taller grass aside, someone was standing in the clearing. He moved closer until the moonlight threw a flicker of light across a beautiful woman with long black hair. She stood in the middle of the field fixated on him. Caught in the hypnotic gaze of her deep blue eyes. Her white dress clinging to her body as a gust of wind blew past her. Slowly she moved closer towards him until she stopped just in front of him. His heart began to race. He felt as if he had seen her before. His palms were damp with sweat, and he rubbed them on his pants. He felt a fluttering inside his chest as he stared into her deep blue eyes. He managed to push the words from his mouth, "Who are you?" She put her finger over his lips and leaned closer to him, until he could feel her lips touching the outer part of his ear. The warmth of her breath blew through him as she whispered something to him. Jason's eyes glazed solid black and in an instant, he was filled with lust. She moved back in front of him as if she were waiting for something, glaring at him with those mesmerizing eyes as she bit her bottom lip. He pulled her in and kissed her passionately. His mind was empty, vacant of everything but her. She pushed her body firmly up against him. Grabbing her firmly, he pulled her to the ground beneath him. He ripped the dress off of her in a frenzy of desire. The moonlight cascaded off her milky white skin and her naked body lay on the ground quivering and calling to him. He was consumed with lust for her.

CLAIRE STARTED to toss and turn while the demon hovered above Jason, its bottom jaw dropped even wider as whispers flooded the air.

THEIR BODIES BECAME ENTWINED on the grassy field. Turning his head, he noticed something moving in the distance. The woman touched her hand to his cheek and brought his head back towards her to regain his attention. He could feel their naked bodies as they pushed against each other. She was like a drug to him, intoxicating every part of his mind. As the thick fog parted slightly in the distance, he heard another rustling in the grass and the sound of sticks breaking. He turned his head again, now closer to him than before, the glare lifted from his eyes and he could see, there was something moving... in the weeds. This time, he was locked in on the shadow of a figure, just beyond the opening in the field. He could hear crows gawking as the flew overhead and through a thinning patch in the fog the figure began to come into focus. The woman again grabbed his cheek and turned his head back towards her, as she once again tried to pull his attention from the sound. Jason could now hear a thousand voices in his head but they were muffled and he couldn't understand what they were saying. She wrapped herself lustfully around him but he could not resist looking back towards the shadow that was still moving in the distant fog. Finally, it was close enough for his eyes to make it out. A tall shadow figure of a man with a top hat stood at the edge of the field and a huge Rottweiler was in the weeds next to him, shaking its head from side to side, holding something in its mouth. As the moonlight broke through the night, a small furry animal came clearly into focus. The dog was viciously gnashing its teeth together and slinging it from side to side, ripping it apart, until finally its flesh collapsed. The blood covered chunk was thrown from the dog's mouth and landed near Jason's side. He jerked his body away from it. The bloody head of a white kitten rolled across the grass and stopped next to his arm. Jerking away quickly, he screamed, and knocked the head away. As he looked back towards the woman, her angelic face contorted into a grotesque demon with bat wings and horns. He let out a horrific scream as he fought to push himself off of her. Her flesh rotted beneath him and her eyes became black as night. Jason's mouth dropped open gasping for air. His eyes widened with fear as every part of his body tensed up. He could feel his heart pounding in his chest as he pushed his hands into the wet ground struggling to free himself from her and catch his breath. There was an intense evil that surrounded him and his body shook. His eyes were locked on the demon and it smiled a wicked grin back at him. He tried to scream but his voice had no sound. He arched his back away from it and tried to pull up onto his knees. The demon's mouth elongated revealing its sharp tarnished teeth as it lashed its snake-like tongue out at him. Jason tried to squirm away, shaking his head from side to side in disbelief. He managed to gain some ground as he clutched the dirt beneath his hands and crawled off the demon. Sweat poured from his face, finally able to catch a breath of air, he pulled himself quickly to his feet. Darting his eyes around the field trying to discern the direction of the house. His naked body was covered with some sort of thick mucus and he slapped his hands all over his skin trying to wipe it off. Just as he turned to see the house in the distance, the demon reached up, grabbed him tightly at the waist and threw him back to ground, slithering on top of him, encasing him beneath its wings. His eyes began to blur as the tears streamed down his face. It grabbed him by the hair pulling his head closer to its mouth as it lunged at him. With a quick gnashing of its teeth, it tore into his flesh, ripping off the lower part of his face. As blood dripped from its mouth, it spit Jason's lower jaw onto the ground and glared up at the sky letting out a long, horrific scream. Jason's body went numb, his eyes rolled back into his head and he began to convulse. He could somehow taste the blood in the back of his throat. Struggling for air, vomit had made its way to what was left of his mouth and poured out the sides of his face. He could no longer cope as the beast sat firmly on top of him, his mind broke apart and everything began to fade to black.

CLAIRE AWAKENED to catch a glimpse of the dark figure leave their room through the open bedroom door. She noticed Jason was covered with sweat, convulsing in his sleep with his mouth wide open.

"Jason!" she cried out, as she shook him.

He let out a huge breath and sat up in bed abruptly, clinching the sheets tightly with his fingers. His eyes wide open, he trembled staring at the blank tv, gasping for air.

"Are you okay?" she asked, as she reached over putting her hand on his arm.

He could barely catch his breath. He flinched and jerked away from her. He was too embarrassed to tell Claire the truth about his dream, nor did he want to repeat it. He had never experienced any nightmare like this before and it felt so real, that it shook him to his core.

He was finally able to mutter, "Yeah, I'm okay. Just, just a bad dream. It's nothing, I'm alright, go back to sleep." He got out of bed, went into the bathroom and splashed water on his face. Staring in the mirror, still feeling numb, he ran his hand over his chin as if to make sure it was still attached.

He didn't want to go back to sleep. He didn't want to risk the chance of the nightmare returning. He walked up the stairs to check on Sara, still pushing the thoughts of the dream out of his mind. He opened her door, looking around the room, he found her sleeping soundly in her bed. He closed the door and glanced around the dimly lit game room. He started to walk down the stairs when he noticed the attic door was slightly open. He walked over, opening the door all the way, trying to look inside the small room. A musty smell poured out, and he couldn't see anything in the dark but shapes of boxes. He closed the door tightly, looking around the game room once more. There was nothing; the house was quiet. Shaking his head and running his fingers through his hair, he fought to drown out the memory of the dream as he walked back down the stairs. It was still playing through his mind no matter how hard he tried to keep his thoughts from it. He walked into the kitchen and shut a cabinet door. "Claire must have left it open after she had cleaned up from dinner," he thought, as he poured a glass of water. He took a deep breath standing over the kitchen sink. He felt numb as the demon's image flashed through his mind. After a few minutes, he returned to their bedroom, trying not to think about it any longer, but it was all he could think about. He stood next to the bed looking at Claire, as she appeared to have fallen back asleep. He walked over to the window and looked out across the lawn into the backyard. In the distance, near the field, he thought he could see something, a shadow. He squinted and moved closer to the window. He couldn't believe what he was seeing, it was sitting still, near the edge of the field staring at him. It was a huge Rottweiler. He blinked his eyes rapidly for a moment and then stared at it intently, almost unable to take his eyes from it. "I must be losing it" he thought. He wiped his hand over his face, closed the curtain and crawled back into bed with Claire.

She rolled over close to him and opened her eyes. "Are you alright?" It was clear to her that he was still visibly shaken.

He fidgeted with the blanket and stared at the ceiling. "I'm fine. It was just... a weird dream. It felt so real. I'm just tired."

Claire sat up in bed and looked at him. "Can I ask you something?"

"Sure," Jason said. He let out a deep breath, rolled over towards her and reached for the remote to turn the television on. He was only partially listening to what she had to say.

She looked at the door and then back towards him, shaking her head slightly. "Earlier tonight, did you open the door?"

"Did I open what door? I don't know," Jason snapped. The frustration of the dream was beginning to get to him, as he flipped through the channels before stopping on a random commercial.

Claire rolled her eyes and lay back down, turning over to face the window and away from Jason. "The bedroom door. I could have sworn I shut it, but when I woke up, it was open," she muttered softly.

He tossed the remote on the nightstand and put his hand on Claire's shoulder, rolling her back towards him. He realized the lump in his throat he was trying to swallow was guilt from the lustful hell he had been plunged into earlier. "I love you, I'm sorry. I just can't think straight." He pulled her closer to him and kissed her. "I'm sorry I snapped at you." He held her to him and she laid her head across his chest, as he wrapped the blanket tightly around them.

Claire closed her eyes but Jason was still fighting the dream out of his mind. He glanced back at the television and started to relax. The commercial had ended and the late-night movie continued to play. The screen was filled with the bloody face of Cujo! Jason's eyes widened as he grabbed the remote and threw it on the floor after turning the television off.

THE ATTIC

The next morning Jason went to work and tried to put the dream out of his mind. He was teaching a class over the summer on art history at the high school. He walked into the front of the school and a woman coming out bumped into him. Her long black hair brushed across his arm.

"Excuse me," the woman said, looking back at Jason and walking quickly towards the parking lot. "I'm sorry," she said again, with another quick glance back at him. She seemed to be in a hurry to get somewhere.

"That's okay," Jason called out. A flash of the woman from his dream went through his mind. It seemed everything throughout the day reminded him of it in one way or another. As he walked in the classroom and set his briefcase on the desk, he couldn't help being a little excited to get back to teaching, if for no other reason than to distract his mind. After all, this was the same high school that he and Claire had actually graduated from. Something about teaching there seemed to make him feel more at ease. The halls and classes hadn't changed that much and he could remember walking with Claire to lunch, and the not-so-great way the cafeteria always seem to smell.

About fifteen eager students awaited his instructions for the day. He sat in the class going over the assignment and glanced out of the window. Sitting in the middle of the parking lot was the black Rottweiler, looking up at him. His face turned a pale white as he got up and walked over to the window in disbelief at what he was seeing. He rubbed his eyes, blinking to clear his vision and looked again. The dog didn't move, and its eyes seem to stare directly at him. He ran his hand over the top of his head and closed his eyes for a couple of seconds, hoping it was gone. However, the dog sat like a statue, staring up at Jason with cold black eyes. He wasn't sure if the dog was real or if it was just an image his brain had clung onto from the dream that had been taunting him all morning.

"Mr. Cole, should we pick one or two subjects for the project?" the student asked. "Mr. Cole?"

"I'm sorry," Jason answered, shaking his head as he turned back towards the class. "One is fine." He looked back out of the window again, but the dog had disappeared. Sitting back down and shifting in his seat, he searched the parking lot over with his eyes, but the dog was nowhere to be seen. He settled back in his chair, leaning over his desk as he watched the time tick by ever so slowly, on the clock at the back of the room. It reminded him maybe a little too much of being in high school on a Friday afternoon and waiting for the sound of that final bell in the last class of the day.

* * *

CLAIRE HAD JUST FINISHED CLEANING up after breakfast, and decided to take Sara outside to play and get some pictures, while the lighting from the sun was still good. She picked out Sara's white shirt with black polka dots, black shorts and black tennis shoes. Picking out outfits to dress her up in was always part of the fun for Claire.

"Come on Sara, it's picture time!" Claire said playfully, as she started to help Sara dress.

"Mommy, I don't want to do pictures again," Sara whined, twisting her hair with her fingers and pushing her bottom lip out into a pout. The life of a CWPP (child with a photographer parent) could be daunting, and Sara was growing less and less cooperative.

"Come on baby, do it for Mommy. Please…" Claire begged, as she fluttered her eyelashes.

Reluctantly, Sara rolled her eyes and sighed, "Okay."

She was full of energy, and the thought of going outside for anything made her smile just a little. She was always daydreaming, pretending with her dolls, or making up new games to play. As an only child, she managed to keep herself entertained. Well, when she wasn't jumping all over Claire, that is.

They went outside in the backyard. It was a beautiful day, as the sunlight's reflection bounced off of the pond. There was a slight breeze in the air, just enough to keep you cooled off from the summer's heat. Everything had turned that full luscious color of green, and with the willow trees hanging down, it looked just like a postcard or a scene out of an old romantic movie. They walked past the pool, which of course made Sara's plans for the day quickly switch to swimming.

"Can we go swimming?" she asked, jumping up and down and swinging around on Claire's waist as if she were a jungle gym.

"Not right now. I want to get some pretty pictures of you by the pond before it gets too hot and I lose the lighting," Claire pleaded. She knew she had to keep Sara interested in taking pictures if she wanted to get a good shot instead of a pout over the loss of her going swimming.

"We can play models, and we can pretend you're a world-famous model and I'm your personal photographer," Claire laughed, twirling around, in an attempt to appeal to Sara's imagination. "Oh Miss Sara, would you please step onto the pier and look back at me, giving me that famous smile of yours?"

"But of course, darling," Sara said, in character. She stepped out onto the pier, tilted her head and gave a cute curtsy while giggling and looking back at Claire.

She skipped farther out onto the end of the pier and again, turned back to look at Claire, throwing one arm into the air. The pond was big and nestled amongst the trees, with a huge field to the right of it. It had always been stocked full of fish, and even though the water was a murky green color, it was calm and peaceful. Claire had spent many summers on that particular pond fishing with Jason. She loved the way the fresh air smelled around her with the wind blowing through the trees.

"Stand right there and give Mommy that pretty smile," Claire said, as she snapped the picture.

After taking several poses, she decided to let Sara play, and started to take pictures of the trees. They really were beautiful the way they swayed in the wind and hung down low towards the ground. As they walked farther away from the house, Sara noticed something moving in the tall grass, beyond the trees and into the field. Claire focused on taking pictures while Sara moved closer towards the movement in the field.

A dark shadow with red eyes moved into the upstairs attic window, starring down at them in the backyard. Claire took several pictures of the flowers and the trees blowing in the wind and Sara soon moved out of sight. Claire could hear a clanging that caught her attention. A chime of some sort. She started following the sound, trying to figure out what it was and where it was coming from.

"Sara," she called out as she glanced back, "don't go far."

She remembered there was an old wooden shack near the pond, where Charlotte used to store fishing poles and tackle. She began to get an uneasy feeling stirring in the pit of her stomach, as she moved closer to the eerie sound. She felt as if someone was watching her. She walked slowly through the grass, looking around and moving closer to the shack. She couldn't see anyone, however it felt as if someone was staring at her every move, and the haunting sound of the chimes gave her a chill. She reached the shed, turned the corner and saw a set of wind chimes hanging from the top of the door and banging up against the wooden frame. She let out a deep breath of air, laughed a little and taking a few steps back, shook her head and snapped a few shots of the wind chimes. She noticed some sort of markings that were carved into the frame of the door that she hadn't remembered being there before. They were odd symbols aligned along the sides and the top of the door frame. She tried to turn the knob and open the door but it was locked. She took a few more pictures and walked back towards the pond feeling a bit foolish that it had frightened her before.

"Sara," she called out, looking towards the pond. Sara was nowhere in sight. The dark shadow stood in the window, its blood-red eyes glaring down at her.

"Sara! Where are you?" Her voice rose and began to shake. She started to run, frantically looking around, but Sara was nowhere in sight. "Sara!" she yelled out.

She ran towards the pond and as she got closer, she fixated on something floating in the water. For a moment everything around her fell silent as if the world itself had come to an abrupt halt. Even her breathing seemed to dissipate as her body froze unable to move. The camera fell out of her hand and hit the ground. Her eyes darted back and forth over the pond. Her mouth opened and short panting breaths began to echo in her head. Slowly she shook her head back and forth until the knot in her stomach formed into a word she was able to force out. "Sara!" she screamed, as every part of her body shook.

Sara's lifeless body was floating in the pond face down, her long blonde hair flowing outward in the water.

"Sara! Sara! Sara!" Claire cried, running as fast as she could with every part of her mind and body trembling.

Sara's arms stretched out from her body floating in the murky water of the pond. Everything was still and even the wind seemed to have stopped blowing. The yard took on a deafening silence and Claire could hear nothing but the sound of her own heart pounding through her chest, as her eyes locked onto Sara's body floating in the pond.

She cried out again, running closer towards the pier, her pulse racing so fast she felt as if she would pass out at any second. As she reached the edge of the pond she tripped over a rock, fell and hit her head hard on the ground. A sharp pain shot through her forehead. She pulled herself up, rubbing her head and opened her eyes; Sara was standing in front of her with a big smile on her face.

"Look mom, I found a kitten!" Sara said, holding a small white kitten and jumping up and down. Claire jerked her head back towards the pond but nothing was there. She looked again at Sara standing dry before her, holding the kitten in her hands. Still visibly shaken, she grabbed Sara and held her tight.

"What's wrong, Mom?" Sara's face saddened.

"Nothing, not a thing baby. Are you okay?" Claire asked, her voice still trembling. She looked at the water and around the yard and back at Sara. She couldn't hold it back any longer, tears rolled down her cheeks, she shook her head back and forth and pulled Sara close to her.

"I'm okay, Mom. Are you okay?" Sara asked, still clinging on to the kitten.

"I don't know, baby," Claire said, her mind still in shock. "I... I don't know."

Claire looked up at the house and caught a glimpse of the dark figure as it moved away from the window. She took a deep breath and got up, picked up Sara and grabbed her camera to go back into the house.

"Mom, look, I found a kitten," Sara said, smiling. She was fighting to hold onto the cat. "Can we keep him? Please?"

"What?" Claire asked, "I don't care." She looked at the house and glanced back at the pond. Her stomach felt sick and she was still confused. Her head was still throbbing from the fall. She couldn't comprehend what she saw, all she knew was, she wanted away from the pond.

She wiped her face and took Sara back into the house. Sara put the kitten down and started to chase it around the house and the cat quickly darted out of sight. Claire picked up the phone and tried to call Jason but it went to his voicemail. "He must still be in class," she thought.

She didn't want to stay in the house either. Her mind was racing with thoughts, trying to rationalize what had happened. "I must be going crazy" she deduced. She kept seeing the image of Sara floating in the water and then the glimpse of the shadow in the window. She had seen flashes of the shadow in the house before. A fleeting shade of darkness out of the corner of her eye, that quickly disappeared when she looked towards it.

"Sara," Claire called out, as she picked up her car keys, "Get your things and come down. We're going into town."

"For pizza?" Sara asked with a huge grin on her face, "I'm hungry."

Sara was like a bottomless pit when it came to eating pizza, chicken nuggets or ice cream, but pizza was by far her favorite. She loved going to the little pizza café in town. They had tables with red checkered table clothes, video arcade games, and a fountain coke machine where she could make her own drink.

"Sounds great," Claire said, as she locked the back door. "Just grab your stuff and come on." Claire walked upstairs to hurry Sara along. She reached the top of the stairs, and noticed the attic door was open.

She looked at Sara fumbling around in her room. "Sara, did

you open that door?" Claire asked as she slowly walked into the game room and approached the attic door.

"No," Sara said, grabbing a few of her toys and shoving them into her backpack to take with her.

Claire stepped inside the door of the attic and turned on the dim light inside the room. It was a small room, quite dusty at this point with a musty smell. The wooden floors creaked as she walked across the attic, towards the window. It faced out into the backyard and had a thin gray curtain hanging over it. An uneasy feeling came over her, as she stepped over old boxes that Charlotte had stored in the room. The attic was surprisingly cold for such a hot afternoon and Claire felt an eerie chill run through her. She made her way to the window, looked out at the back yard, and thought about the shadow she saw earlier. The pond demanded her attention as the image of Sara floating stuck in her mind. A deep scratching noise came from the other side of the room, like nails scrapping slowly across the wooden floor. She jerked her head towards the sound but the scratching stopped as soon as she looked. Claire's pulse quickened, she ran her hand across her forehead and noticed it more difficult to breath. She walked slowly to the other side of the room, trying to locate where the noise had come from. There was a stack of boxes pushed up against the wall and again she heard the sound of clawing from behind the boxes. She reached down and moved the boxes out of the way to find a small door with a padlock on it. She reached for the old lock when she heard the slow clawing sound again, but this time it was on the opposite side of the room from her. She jerked her head back in that direction and the noise, once again, stopped. Her breathing became more rapid and her skin began to feel as if something was crawling on her. She brushed off her arms and focused back on the small locked door that she had discovered. She glanced around the room again and in the dim light she noticed a dark figure standing in the room, just inside the attic door.

Startled, she let out a horrific scream. Sara jumped and tripped over her backpack, falling backwards onto the floor in the attic, crying.

"Sara!" Claire shouted. "What are you doing in here?" She rushed over to help her up.

Sara was still crying and rubbing her eyes. "Mom, you scared me."

"I'm sorry, you scared me. Let's get out of here," Claire said, nervously looking around the room. She took Sara's hand, turned out the light and shut the attic door behind them.

They headed into town for pizza and to get out of the house for a while. Claire tried to call Jason again, however, it was still going to his voicemail. She couldn't stop her mind from thinking about everything. "Maybe the noise in the attic was a rat. What was that locked door? Maybe the pond was, I don't know... a brain tumor." She drove into town in somewhat of a daze, as her mind struggled to rationalize things. "Maybe I didn't see anything at all and my eyes were just playing tricks on me. It was just for a few seconds. Fear can make you see or think you see anything. I was worried when I couldn't find Sara. The door..." Claire kept shoveling through her thoughts until she finally pushed it from her mind.

They parked the car in the big parking lot at the end of Main Street and walked down to the little pizza café. For a little while Claire was able to get her mind off of the day as Sara pulled her attention in every direction.

"Let's play the shooting game!" Sara suggested, as they walked in the cafe. She couldn't hit anything, but she liked holding the gun that was almost bigger than she was and aiming at the ducks. The smell of pizza filled the air and it was a welcoming break in the day for Claire.

"Okay," Claire said, smiling down at her. She would rather let Sara keep her busy than letting her mind rest on thoughts of the pond and the locked door in the attic.

After they ate their pizza, they started to walk down Main Street when Claire saw the hardware store. It brought back memories for her from when she was younger. It was a small family owned store with the famous red door, which had a sign hanging over it that read, 'Peterson's Hardware', with a picture of a toolbox and a hammer. It was owned by an elderly couple that had a son and a daughter, Tom and Gabby. Gabby had moved away to open up her own business in a nearby town while Tom, who had gone to school with Jason and Claire, chose to stay behind and eventually take over the family business. After all, Tom was somewhat responsible for the success of the store. It was the only shop with a solid red door, which made it easy to spot on Main Street and in truth, it was an accident that it came to be red. When Tom was younger, he painted the entire bottom half of the door with dark red paint. It was so difficult to paint over, that old man Peterson decided to just paint the entire door red. In spite of all the trouble Tom got into over it, the store became well known as, 'The Red Door Hardware Store'. Eventually, it actually boosted business and made the store famous throughout the West Feliciana parish. It's odd how something that seemed to make the old man so mad at the time, could turn out to be such a blessing in disguise. For now, Tom and his father worked side by side and owning the famous hardware store guaranteed a profitable return for both of them.

"Sara, come on. Mommy wants to pick up a few things." Claire held the red door open for Sara.

"I love the red door, it's so pretty!" Sara said, jumping up and down and spinning in circles.

"Yeah, that's a funny story," Claire smirked. "When you're older, I'll tell it to you."

They walked into the store and Claire picked up a couple of large rat traps and placed them on the counter.

"Claire?" A tall man with broad shoulders stepped out from behind the counter. "Oh my gosh, it's so great to see you. I heard you and Jason were back in town. I'm so sorry about Charlotte, she was so sweet."

Claire recognized Tom right away, even though it had been years since she last seen him, "Thank you." She gave him a friendly hug. "It's good to see you too. Jason is teaching over at the high school. You have to come out to the house and see us. We've only been back a few months but getting settled in has just been crazy."

Just then Pastor Gabriel from Sunnyside Church walked into the store.

"Claire Cole!" the pastor said, with a big grin. He was your typical Louisiana pastor, an old man with grey hair and a beard who always had a big smile on his face and a cheerful personality. He had been the pastor for Sunnyside church as long as she could remember, and had married Jason and Claire shortly after college.

"How have you been?" he asked, as he shook her hand tight. "Who might this little angel be?" he asked with a smile, looking down at Sara and patting her on the head.

"This is mine and Jason's daughter, Sara," Claire said, smiling. "Sara, this is Pastor Gabriel from church, he is a friend of ours. It's so wonderful to see you again, sir."

"Hi," Sara said, looking up at Gabriel and then quickly turning her attention to the small row of candy in front of the counter.

"Hello to you, young lady, nice to meet you. Tom, how are you today?" Gabriel asked, glancing over at Tom and giving him a friendly nod. "Can you get me some of those special light bulbs I use in the sanctuary please?"

"Sure thing, sir," Tom said, turning around and walking into the back of the store.

"I have been meaning to come by since the funeral and check on the both of you. How are you getting settled in at the house?" Gabriel asked, turning his attention back to Claire.

"Oh, everything is… fine," Claire said with a slight hesitation as she nervously turned the wedding ring repeatedly on her finger.

He noticed her fidgeting and gave her a concerned look but smiled anyway.

He tilted his head and raised his eyebrows, "Are you sure everything is okay?" Giving her another opportunity to say whatever it was; he knew she was holding back.

"Yes. I mean, moving and everything I guess, just stress. I'm sure everything is fine," Claire replied, as she directed her fidgeting to the rat traps she had placed on the counter. "I think we may have some rats."

"Well, if you ever need anything, my door is always open," the pastor said, and he wrote his number down on a piece of paper and handed it to Claire. "You call me should anything come up. Even if you just need someone to talk too. Take care of this little one and I'll expect to see all three of you in church on Sunday," he winked and chuckled a bit, looking down at Sara.

Just then Tom returned with the set of light bulbs and placed them on the counter and Gabriel handed him the money. "Tom, how's your dad doing?" he asked.

"Oh fine, sir," Tom smiled back at Gabriel and put the light bulbs in a bag.

"What about your sister? We haven't heard from her in some time."

"Gabby? She's great. Her business has really picked up but she's still single. I don't suppose she will ever get past losing that boyfriend she had," Tom looked down at the counter to avoid eye contact with Claire.

"That was a tragic thing. We lost a lot of people that year," Gabriel reached out and shook Tom's hand. I'll see you folks Sunday."

Tom smiled and shot Claire a quick glance, "Absolutely. You have a nice day, pastor."

"Will do, and tell your father I said hello." Gabriel turned to walk towards the door of the store, looking back once more at Claire. "Claire, Sara, let me know if you need anything."

"Thank you," Claire smiled. Her mind was switching back and forth from the conversation to everything that had happened that morning. Inside her head, a voice was screaming out, "I may be losing my mind! I think I saw something in the pond, and maybe in the house! Please help me!"

"It was great seeing you again," she said, pushing her thoughts aside. "Stop by the house sometime. I know Jason would love to see you."

Pastor Gabriel left and walked down the street back towards the church. Claire started to pay when she looked over and saw a doorknob kit with a lock. She picked it up and put it on the counter.

"This too, please. Oh, do you have anything that will cut a lock?" she asked.

"I have a pair of bolt cutters that should work." He reached behind the counter and grabbed the bolt cutters.

Claire saw a closed door just beyond the counter. It had symbols marked on the frame right towards the bottom and one above the door much like the ones she had seen on the shack.

"And this?" Sara asked as she put a candy bar on the counter.

"Okay," Claire said, "but that's it," still staring at the markings on the door. "Tom, what was all that about your sister?"

He shook his head and began to put her things in a bag. "Oh Gabby, it was a long time ago. We were all still pretty young, as a matter of fact she wasn't much more than about sixteen. She lost her boyfriend in a car accident. She never got over it. It was a strange year. A virus broke out and a lot of people got sick, some died. It was just a bad deal." He handed her the bag and smiled. "But, like I said, that was a long time ago."

"I remember that," Claire said, picking up the bolt cutters off the counter. "All the businesses in town shut down for months trying to control the virus. My dad kept me in the house."

"Like I said, it was a bad deal. Gabby lost Kyle just before the virus broke out but, she is okay now. Claire, tell Jason hello for me and tell him stop by and see me soon." He cut the conversation off and glanced back at the door.

"Oh, I will, and don't be a stranger," Claire replied, handing him the money and trying not to stare at the symbols. "Bye Tom." She waved, and as they walked out of the store. She opened Sara's candy and handed it to her.

"Here you go, but what you don't finish by the time we get to the car, it's going in the trash. Agree?" She wasn't actually giving Sara much of a choice.

"Agree," Sara said. She was used to not being able to eat or drink in the car, so she quickly ate her candy bar as not to waste a single bit of chocolate.

They drove home and the first thing Claire did after they arrived at the house, was to go upstairs to the attic and replace the old doorknob. She felt a sense of control now that the attic door locked, and would no longer open unless she opened it. She stepped inside the attic and pushed the boxes out of the way to reveal the hidden door. Clinching the bolt cutters around the lock, she squeezed with all her strength but the lock stayed firmly in place. Finally she gave up, turned out the light and shut the attic door. She turned the knob to make sure it was locked. "I'll have to get Jason's help." As she turned around, Sara was standing next to the pool table looking flustered.

"Mommy, I can't find the kitten," Sara cried, and she began running around the house from room to room.

"He must have got out. I'll help you look tomorrow."

"But... I want the cat," Sara whined, as she ran down the stairs continuing her search.

"Maybe he has another home, and he was just here visiting,"

Claire said, trying to comfort her, "I bet he will come visit us another day."

Sara gave into the thought and wiped her eyes, "Okay."

* * *

THAT EVENING after Jason returned home, they sat down for dinner.

"How was school?" Claire looked at Jason, wondering if he had seen all of her missed calls.

"Oh, it was okay. Not that many students. I'm sure once the new year starts it will be much better. So strange to be back in that school again. Brought back a lot of memories of me chasing around the most beautiful girl on campus," he gave her a wink. "How was your day? Anything interesting happen?"

"We went for pizza!" Sara said, before Claire could get a chance to speak, "And I got to shoot ducks and I was a model!"

"Well, that sounds fun," Jason noticed Claire was staring down and picking at her food. "Claire? Everything okay?"

"Yes, pizza... It was fun," she answered, nodding her head at Sara before glancing back at Jason. "I tried to call you several times."

"And Mommy showed me the red door," Sara interrupted excitedly, as she shoved another bite of food in her mouth.

"Nice. You guys go to the hardware store today?" he looked at Claire. He noticed she was upset about something. "What for?"

She let out a deep sigh and decided to put the conversation on hold until Sara was in bed. "Just to pick up a couple of things. I saw Tom. He said to tell you hello," she looked back at her food and took another bite of mashed potatoes.

"What did you need from the hardware store?" He noticed Claire's distant attitude.

She hesitated for a moment, "Um, just a few things for around the house. Light bulbs and stuff."

"Okay," He thought it best to drop the subject assuming she was still upset about the phone calls. He had meant to call her back but lost track of time. He had his own haunting thoughts of the day.

CLAIRE PUT Sara to bed after dinner. When she returned back to their bedroom, she couldn't hold back any longer. She told Jason everything that had happened to her that day with the pond and the shadow she thought she saw in the attic. "Didn't you see my missed calls? Jason, I heard sounds in the attic and there is a door inside with a bolt on it and…"

"Claire, I'm sure it's okay. There has to be a reasonable explanation," Jason pulled his pajamas on. "This old house can make you stir crazy. Maybe you need to put Sara in a daycare program for the summer and try and get some work done. You know, get your mind off things. I heard the mayor was looking for someone to take photos of the town for the new website to promote tourism. Maybe you should go talk to him. I'm sure you would love to be back in the darkroom developing again." He reached over to pull her close to him but she pulled away.

"What about the door with the lock?" she asked.

"This house has been in my family for a long time. Back then they use to build them with extra doors in the attic. Probably just to reach the cooling system or something. I'm sure my grandmother probably put the bolt on it for safety, so no one would go in there. You see how she put bolts on doors around here. Everything is okay Claire, I promise," he tried to reassure her. "I think your imagination is just starting to mess with you a bit. You need to get out of the house. Call the mayor. Check on the job."

Claire picked at her nails relentlessly. "I suppose you're right.

When I say it out loud, it sounds ridiculous. As much as I love being with Sara, I would love to work again. I haven't had much time to work in darkroom since we converted it."

"Then that settles it," Jason said. "In the morning, sign Sara up and go talk to the mayor about the job." He pulled Claire close. "So, you really changed the doorknob upstairs?" he smirked.

Claire playfully hit him and they rolled around on the bed laughing.

"It was really scary," she said with a smile as she stopped and laid her head on Jason's chest. "But seriously, Jason, the pond thing with Sara... I mean, I just can't... I don't know what I would do if anything ever happened to her."

"Nothing is going to happen. I'm sorry I didn't call you back today." Jason held her close until they finally fell asleep.

THE BOOKSTORE

*T*he next day Claire went into town and enrolled Sara at daycare for the summertime fun program. Sara was excited to be around other kids her own age and Claire was anxious to get back to work again and put everything out of her mind. After speaking to the mayor, he was more than happy to hire Claire on the spot for the town project. She had been working on community events since they had returned and was easily the best photographer around.

Claire knew the town well and it looked the same as it had when they left. She loved the old-style grace of the buildings' architecture and the feel of the shops that lined the streets. As she walked up Main Street, she took pictures of the different storefronts and the people walking in and out of the little shops. When she came to the bookstore, she stopped and went in. It was a small shop lined with shelves full of different types of books. There was a counter that stretched out across the back of the store and two small white tables with chairs nestled in the corners for readers to sit and enjoy their books. She started to glance through the books, when she noticed a man walk into the store and approach the woman at the counter in the back. He looked nervous for some reason, and although Claire didn't consider herself the nosy type, it did catch her attention. The woman behind the counter was an older, attractive black woman and she gave Claire a slight glance when she noticed her paying a little too much attention to their conversation. Claire quickly turned back to the books. The woman stepped through a door behind the counter and returned with a black cloth bag and handed it to the man, who paid and then left the store. Claire thought it odd and stepped outside the shop and watched the man walk away. "What was in the bag?" she wondered. As he got into his car, Claire held up her camera and snapped a picture.

"Did you find everything you were looking for?" the woman asked, as she stepped out of the store.

Claire jumped. "Oh I'm sorry, um yes, I was just... looking around. Thank you."

"Kristina Graves," the woman said, as she held out her hand to Claire. "I own this shop. And you are?"

"Oh, Claire," she said nervously, shaking her hand in return. "Claire Cole. I just moved back into town a few months ago with my husband and I'm taking some pictures for the mayor. I'm sorry, I didn't mean to..."

"Cole?" Kristina asked. "Are you Charlotte's grandson, Jason's wife?"

"Yes," Claire said, surprised.

"My goodness," Kristina smiled. "I was a very close friend of Charlotte, and I knew her daughter Cindy as well. God rest their souls".

Claire let out a breath of relief and laughed. "Oh, thank God," she said. "For a minute, I was freaking out."

"Nonsense," Kristina said. "Why, any family of Charlotte and Cindy is always welcome around here. Come on into the shop and I'll pour us a cup of tea."

They walked into the shop and Claire sat at one of the small white round tables in the corner of the store. Kristina went into the back and quickly returned with two cups of hot tea and four beignets.

"I haven't had a chance to go by the house since it all happened," Kristina said sadly, as she sat down and took a sip of tea. "I just haven't been able to bring myself to go back there after finding her."

"You're the one that found Charlotte?" Claire asked.

"Yes, unfortunately. She used to help with some things around the shop and when she didn't show up, I went to her house and that's when I found her. Just an awful thing to lose such a wonderful woman. I've known Charlotte since I first moved to town. As a matter of fact, she is the one that encouraged me to buy this bookstore and make it my own. I miss her. How are you and Jason? You have a small child too? A daughter; is that right?" Kristina asked.

"Yes, Sara, she is five and a handful but she is enjoying living here very much," Claire said. "And Jason is teaching at the high school and I'm just sorry we weren't down here more. It seems like it always takes something like a tragedy to realize how important it is to make time for family."

"I understand. Charlotte was the closest thing to family in this town that I had. Why, I couldn't even bring myself to walk over to the graveside at the funeral. And you? How are you doing here?" Kristina asked, sitting back in her chair.

"Oh, you know. I'm okay. The service was lovely, she would have liked all the people that showed up" Claire replied, still fidgeting with her beignet.

"Yes, she would have. I watched from the road, but the turnout was nothing less than she deserved. She had so many friends here in town," she looked at Claire. "Not much to do in this old town. I've had to resign myself to the fact that at fifty-three I'm probably going to be an old maid."

They both laughed. It was nice for Claire to have someone to talk to other than Sara.

"Hey, can I ask you something strange?" Claire said, a little hesitant to tell her new friend anything about the situation in the house. She knew it sounded crazy, and this was the first time she had been able to sit down with anyone that wasn't five years old and have any type of conversation.

"Sure," Kristina said, taking another sip of tea.

"The hardware store; do you know the owners very well?" Claire asked. She was trying to figure out a way to ask the question that was burning in the back of her mind, without sounding too nosy.

"The Petersons? Yes, I know Mr. Peterson and his son Tom very well. They are good shop neighbors to have. Why do you ask?" Kristina said.

"I was over there today and I noticed these weird symbols on one of the doors behind the counter. I saw some out at our place too that looked kind of the same and I was just wondering what they were. Did you happen to notice them when you were in the store?" She tried not to look too suspicious.

"No, I can't say that I have," Kristina said, looking curiously at Claire, "You know a lot of these people put harvest symbols up for good luck with their business. Maybe that's all it is. People do weird things in this town."

Claire shook it off and felt a little ridiculous for asking; she hoped she didn't look like a complete fool. She stayed there and talked to Kristina for about an hour before she moved on with her day and continued to take pictures of the town. After she had all the shots she needed, she went to pick Sara up from daycare and the symbols on the door became nothing more than a distant thought.

"How was your day?" Claire asked as she reached down and hugged Sara tightly.

"I love it! I made new friends," Sara said excitedly. She

jumped into the back seat of the car throwing her things on the seat.

"That's great. How would you like to go home and help me make dinner for Daddy?" Claire asked.

"Yes! Yes!" Sara said, buckling her seatbelt and situating herself.

Claire and Sara drove home and went into the house to start dinner. They worked together to make a pot of spaghetti, and when Jason got home they all sat down to eat and talk about their day.

"Claire, did you get a chance to talk to the mayor about the job?" Jason asked.

"Oh, yes. As a matter of fact, I started today. I think I needed out of the house more than I thought. I got some great shots of Main Street," Claire answered, as she continued to eat.

"And I made new friends today, Daddy!" Sara interrupted, bouncing a little in her chair.

"You did? That's great," Jason replied, looking over at her.

"And we colored pictures and went outside and played and sang songs and ate donuts!"

"Well, sounds like you both had a good day," Jason said.

"Oh, I met the lady from the..." Claire started, but Sara quickly interrupted her again.

"Mom, can I go back tomorrow? We are supposed to plant flowers!" Sara asked, picking the last meatball out of her food and shoving it in her mouth.

"Yes, I think that's a plan," Claire gave Sara a wink. "I better clean you up, you have spaghetti all over you. Go upstairs and start your bath and I'll be up in a minute."

"Okay," Sara said, getting up from the table and running up the stairs.

Claire picked up their plates and started to clean up the kitchen. "Jason, the locked door... Do you think you can cut the bolt off? I'm curious."

"I had a long day at school today," Jason said, putting his plate in the sink. "I'm going to hop in the shower, I'll get to it this weekend. It's nothing." He kissed Claire on the cheek and went into their bedroom.

Claire finished cleaning up and went upstairs to help Sara with her bath and tuck her in for the night.

"All done?" she asked Sara, handing her a towel.

"Yes Mommy," she replied, looking up at Claire and getting out of the tub.

Claire helped her put on her nightgown and tucked her into bed. "Goodnight love."

"Dragonfly!" Sara cried.

"I'm sorry," Claire reached over and handed Sara the dragonfly from the shelf.

She closed the bedroom door and as she started to walk down the stairs, she noticed the attic door was open. She stood at the top of the stairs, looking intently at the door. Once again, that uneasy feeling washed over her, and she walked slowly through the game room and towards the attic door. Her breathing became shallow, as thoughts of putting on the new lock ran through her mind. As she reached for the knob, the light came on inside the attic room. She slammed the door shut quickly and stood still unable to move, staring at the door. After a few seconds she reached for the knob and tried to open the door, but it was locked. She pulled and jerked on the door, but it wouldn't open. She backed up, still staring at the door, and from underneath, through the crack at the floor, she could see the light, then it suddenly went off again. Claire gasped, and backed up slowly to Sara's room. She opened Sara's bedroom door to look at her once more, before closing it back again and walking downstairs to her own bedroom. She crawled into bed and sat very still until Jason came out of the bathroom.

"What's wrong?" Jason asked, after he stepped out of the bathroom drying his head with a towel.

"The door..." Claire said, still trying to catch her composure. "It was open."

Jason started to dress for bed and glanced back at Claire, "What door?"

"The attic door, the fucking attic door was open!" Claire cried, starting to panic.

"Hey, calm down. I'm sure it's just the pressure from the air conditioner or something. You know, when it comes on it probably had pressure built up and just pushed it open," Jason explained, as he finished putting on his pajamas. He climbed into bed next to Claire.

"It was locked! I put the lock on myself! Are you listening to me? The light came on inside the room and I shut the door and then it wouldn't open. Then the light went off! Jason, something's wrong!"

He shook his head, "Claire, you're not making any sense. The door probably wasn't closed all the way the first time, and if the light flickered it was probably the power. You're overreacting." He reached over and switched the light off.

"It was closed," Claire said. She was getting more agitated by the minute. "It was closed and locked."

Jason sat up in bed and looked at Claire. "Claire, think about it. It had to be slightly open before. The air probably just pushed it all the way open when the AC kicked on. Did you shut it back?"

"Yes," Claire replied, shaking her head. "But..."

"Did you make sure it was closed this time?" He smirked.

"Yes, I yanked the shit out of it!" She pushed her hair back from her face.

"Then I'm sure no boogie man is going to open it. Come on, get some sleep," Jason said anxiously as he rolled over, dismissing her.

Claire couldn't sleep, she didn't like it when Jason blew everything off that she had to say, like she was nothing more than a scared schoolgirl. She kept thinking about the attic door. She turned on the television to try and distract her mind. Jason fell asleep quickly, and his snoring got on her nerves a little more than usual. Finally, she was able to fall asleep until about one in the morning, when she was awakened by a loud noise. As she lay there listening intently, she heard it again. Bam. Bam. Bam. Heavy footsteps stomped across the attic floor above them.

"Jason," Claire whispered. "Jason, wake up." She leaned over and shook Jason's shoulder. She heard the stomping again, like boots hitting the hardwood floors in the attic.

"Jason! Wake up! I hear something."

He sat up in bed. "What is it?" he rubbed his eyes as he pulled himself awake.

"Shhhh. Listen," she said, and the room fell silent.

Jason didn't hear anything. "Claire, what is it?" He looked at her and glanced back around the room. "Did you hear Sara?"

"I heard something. It sounded like someone stomping around in the attic," She tried to hold her breath as not to make any noise.

"Claire… You were probably dreaming. What time is it? Ugh, it's one o'clock in the morning. You're really freaking yourself out. Try and get some sleep," Jason plopped back down on his pillow exasperated.

He rolled over, jerking the covers up and went back to sleep. Claire lay awake staring at the ceiling. She realized he wouldn't believe anything she had to say at this point. He was clearly frustrated. She listened for the noise until finally she fell back to sleep.

About 3:15 in the morning, the attic door creaked slowly open and a dark shadow of a man with a tall hat emerged and stood in front of Sara's door. The doorknob began to slowly turn, and the door pushed open, as the shadowy figure moved into Sara's room and stood next to her bed, staring down at her.

It began to run its pointy fingers through Sara's long blonde hair, and with a low voice it whispered, "Soon." The dark shadow left Sara's bedside and moved through the house, into Jason and Claire's room. As it looked at both of them this time, it moved towards Claire's side of the bed. The dark figure moved above Claire's body and as it tilted its head upward, its mouth dropped wide open and whispers filled the air. Claire began to toss and turn, and a thousand voices flooded her thoughts as she began to dream.

She was standing in the middle of town taking pictures when she noticed Sara standing at the end of the street in the middle of the road. "Sara," she called out, but Sara didn't turn around. She could hear something coming in the distance and as she turned, she saw a truck speeding down the road, coming straight at Sara.

"Sara!" She rushed towards her daughter just in time to push her out of the road, then all at once she found herself lying on a table covered with a sheet saturated with blood. She couldn't move and fear overtook her. She could see something on top of her, on top of the sheet, but she couldn't make it out. She started to gasp for air but the sheet was tight and she could smell the stench of blood covering her.

The demon floated above Claire whispering as she slept.

She tried to cry out for help but nothing would come out of her mouth. All she could see was the shape of something on top of her. A hole ripped through the sheet just above her right eye. She looked frantically around the room out of the open hole, trying to focus on anything she could see, when a long finger with rotten flesh reached through the hole and a sharp fingernail pierced into her eye. She screamed out as her body trembled and her eye sank heavily back into her skull. The room fell upon a deafening silence and an eerie voice through the sound of rushing water whispered, "Claire." She tried to scream again but nothing came out, and the demon took its long fingers and ran its nails down her body. "He is coming Claire," the voice continued to whisper. She could feel its hand touching her and everything in her wanted it to stop but it didn't. Its nails began to cut deep into her flesh as it ran its hand down her body and blood poured out of her skin, dripping onto the floor. Claire screamed inside, "Jesus, help me!" The demon stopped and stared at her. Blood oozed from her eye socket and she tried with everything she could to get the words out of her mouth, but nothing would come. The demon continued to run his hands slowly over her, slicing her flesh with its fingernails. Her blood ran over her legs and dripped from the table. She tried to cry out again and finally using every bit of strength she had, she was able to say one word, "Jesus!" The demon moved away from Claire and stared down at her. "Jesus!" Claire screamed again, louder and stronger than before and the demon vanished.

THE DEMON STOPPED and moved off of Claire, it lingered for a moment and then crept back out of the bedroom and into the night.

Claire awoke, gasping for air and shaking as she reached up touching her eye. "Jason!" It took her a few minutes before she could tell him about her dream. Even though he was annoyed at being woken up again, he tried to comfort her. He knew how disturbing some of those dreams could be, after all he was still feeling the aftereffects from his own nightmare.

"It's okay, Claire," he said, trying to calm her down. "It was just a bad dream. Probably because we were talking about all that stuff before we went to sleep."

"I'm going to check on Sara," she was getting a little tired of

Jason's dismissive attitude and was trying to put the nightmare out of her head. She didn't want to go back to sleep, or lie in the bed next to Jason at this minute. She got up and went upstairs. The first thing she did was look at the attic door, which was still closed, much to her relief. She opened Sara's bedroom door to find her still peacefully asleep, clinging on to the dragonfly. She crawled into bed with her and held her tightly until she was able to fall back asleep. She slept peacefully for the rest of the night, and nothing returned to bother her again.

MARKED

The sun was bright without a cloud in the sky and the wind blew a soft breeze through the trees in the bayou. The glorious smell of charcoal burning filled the backyard as Jason put the burger patties on the grill. Green and blue balloons with streamers hung around the patio and a strawberry cake with a white and blue number '6' candle sat front and center on the table. One by one, Sara's friends from daycare showed up with colorful wrapped packages, and soon they were all splashing in the pool pretending to be hungry sharks. Claire pushed the thoughts of the house from her mind and focused on capturing the memories of the day with her camera.

"Jason," a familiar voice called out. It was Pastor Gabriel. "I knocked on the front door but I guess you folks couldn't hear me. I hope you don't mind me coming around, I heard all the little ones splashing in the pool and thought it best to walk back and say hello."

"Of course not. It's great seeing you again," Jason said. "I'm glad you stopped by, just in time for a burger. It's Sara's birthday; she turned six today."

"Pastor Gabriel, so nice of you to stop by," Claire said,

reaching out and shaking his hand. "Would you like a glass of tea?"

"Thank you, that would be nice," He took a seat next to the pool. "My, they grow up so fast. I don't want to interrupt your party, I just wanted to check on you folks and see how things were going."

"No not at all. You're welcome here any time." Jason placed layers of cheese on each burger patty.

Gabriel couldn't help but notice Claire staring towards the field. She had the same expression of desperation on her face that she did in the hardware store, which was why he had decided to pay a visit. Claire shifted nervously in her seat and looked back at the house. The vacant window in the attic seemed to always be watching her. She looked back at Gabriel and smiled politely.

"You alright?" Gabriel asked.

"Of course," Claire replied, turning back to watch Sara splashing in the pool.

Jason pulled Gabriel's attention quickly back to him, as he took the burgers off of the grill. "It's been so busy around here getting the house back into shape but I think we're finally there. Sara loves it here. How are things with you?"

"Blessed. I have no complaints" Gabriel said, looking back at Jason. "I'm glad y'all are getting settled in."

Jason's rambling about fishing faded slowly to the background as Gabriel looked back at the house to see, if anything, what Claire was looking at before. Turning back towards Jason he caught a glimpse out of the corner of his eye, a shadow moved across the attic window. He quickly jerked his head back but the fleeting darkness disappeared and he thought no more of it than an old man's mind.

"Did you see something?" Claire asked. She couldn't help but notice the expression on his face and was desperate for validation of her own sanity.

"What?" Gabriel asked. "Oh no, just an old man's eyes playing tricks."

Jason quickly changed the subject, "Claire, can you get the towels from the house? The food is about ready and the kids are going to need to dry off to eat."

"Sure," Claire said, getting up and walking towards the house.

"Well, I have to be going too. I'll let you folks get back to your party," Gabriel turned back towards the house. "Claire, I'll walk with you, if you don't mind? Jason, it was a pleasure. See you in church tomorrow?" He reached out to shake Jason's hand and looked over at the kids in the pool. "Hey! Happy Birthday Sara!"

"Wouldn't miss it," Jason replied. "Drive safe."

Gabriel stopped and turned back at Jason one last time, "Oh, better put your dog on a leash, especially with these kids out here. Folks around town have gotten funny about that."

Jason's face turned a pale color as he pulled the last burger off the grill and stared back at the pastor. "What dog?"

"Big black dog, hanging around in front. I assumed it was yours," he continued to walk into the house with Claire. "See you tomorrow."

The pastor's words hung in the air and Jason froze and everything around him faded but the image of the dog. He peered around the side of the house to the front lawn but the dog was nowhere to be seen. "Has to be a stray," he thought, his eyes searching for any sign of the creature lurking about. "It can't be the same dog."

"Everyone out of the pool," Jason snapped, looking back towards the kids and taking a deep breath. "It's time to eat." He glanced once again towards the front of the house.

* * *

Gabriel noticed Claire was extra quiet stepping into the house. Her eyes were bloodshot and she looked as if she hadn't slept in days.

"Claire, I can't shake this feeling that something is bothering you," he said. "I've known you and your family a long time. I know how hard it was for you after your dad passed away. Please, if there is something wrong, maybe I can help. You can talk to me."

Claire looked up at him and shook her head. "It's stupid when I say it out loud. I mean it sounds ridiculous." She laughed for a moment and stopped. "Whenever it actually comes out of my mouth and I hear myself… it's no wonder Jason thinks I'm losing it."

Gabriel reached over and took hold of her hand, "If it's upsetting you this much, it's not stupid."

She took a deep breath, "It's this house. I have been having nightmares and they are so realistic. I've never had dreams like this before. And the pond, the other day…" She stopped and wiped a tear from her face and shook her head. "The attic… the door keeps opening and I found a hidden door up there with a bolt on it. I tried to get it off but I couldn't and Jason still hasn't tried to unlock it. He dismisses everything, like it's nothing. There are footsteps at night. I can hear them and the kitchen cabinets are always open! I shut them all day but still they're open!"

Gabriel's eyes narrowed and he sat back in the chair, "Claire, I'm not sure I understand you."

"The house. There is something in this house," she murmured softly.

He leaned forward taking her hand, "Claire, this house has been here for years. All houses hold their secrets. Old houses creak and shift which can cause doors to open, and some doors are better left locked."

Claire pulled her hand away and shifted in the chair, "What are you talking about? This is more than an unsettled house."

Gabriel got up and wiped the sweat off his forehead and started to walk towards the front door.

"Wait! You don't understand," she pleaded.

He turned and whispered softly, "The more attention you give them, the more they will give you. God is stronger. Have faith and call upon Him. He will help you. I have to leave, I'm sorry."

"Wait, please. I don't understand ," she reached out to grab hold of his hand. A loud noise came from upstairs like something heavy had fallen on the wooden floor.

Gabriel jerked his head towards the ceiling. "I have to go. I'm sorry Claire. Come by my office after church. We can talk more then. I'll help you, but not here." He started to walk out of the house, but stopped one last time to see the desperate look on her face. He leaned over to her and whispered, "Something is drawing it here. Something dark. You need to find out what's causing that open door and shut it for good. And Claire, do so quietly. Ignore it best you can, pay it no attention. It's watching you." and he walked out of the house.

She looked up at the ceiling one last time before grabbing the towels to carry outside. The children were sitting around the pool finishing up their burgers when she reached them.

"Where have you been?" Jason asked, still looking anxiously towards the front yard. "Stand here and watch Sara and the kids."

"Why? What's going on?" Claire asked, as she watched Jason sprint towards the front yard.

Jason ran around to the front of the house and looked up and down the street. All he could see was the taillights of Gabriel's car as he drove out of sight. Jason began to whistle, "Here puppy, puppy! Come on puppy! You bastard." There was no dog in sight and Jason walked back around the house and slumped down in the chair next to Claire.

"What are you doing?" her voice was still a bit shaky thinking of the words Gabriel had left her with.

"Nothing," Jason said. "Chasing a figment of my imagination."

"Jason, I tried to talk to Pastor Gabriel about what's been going on in the house, but..."

"Claire! why would you do that? I told you it was nothing! You want the people in this town talking about the crazy family that's back!" Jason got up and gathered the empty plates from the kids.

"Jason, he isn't going to say anything. He didn't think I was crazy. He..."

Claire was interrupted by Sara jumping up and down. "Can we have cake now!"

"Sure, yes. Let's do the cake," Claire said, looking at Jason.

They sang 'Happy Birthday' while the other kids gathered around, anxiously awaiting a piece of cake.

Once all the kids were served cake and ice cream, Claire sat down next to Jason. "I'm sorry." She wanted to tell him the strange conversation she had with Gabriel but she could tell he was miles away from listening.

Jason dazed off into the field and finished his cake. All he could think about was the image of the black dog.

After the party ended and all the children were picked up, Claire bathed Sara and they put on a movie that she had gotten for her birthday. They had promised to watch one with her before she went to bed, and Sara made sure they remembered. She sat on the floor of the living room playing with her new toys as quickly as Jason could tear them out of the boxes, and she sang along to every song in the movie as if she were the star herself. "It must be nice to be six," Jason thought, still struggling to get the last tea set loose from the box. Claire cleaned everything up, and finally the day wore Sara out, and she passed out asleep on the floor.

"I'll put her in bed," Jason said, as he picked her up and started for the stairs.

Claire turned everything off and went in her room to lie down. Her thoughts were still hanging on the words that Gabriel had spoken to her earlier, until she finally fell asleep. It had been a long day for all of them. Jason crawled into bed next to her and for the first time in a while they slept through the night.

* * *

THE NEXT MORNING, they were up bright and early, heading to church. It was another pretty day outside, without a cloud in the sky. As service came to an end, Pastor Gabriel stood at the entrance of the church and shook everyone's hand as they left one by one. When Jason reached the pastor, he shook his hand but was pulled aside momentarily. "Would you mind waiting?"

Jason fidgeted with his keys while the pastor finished greeting everyone, until the church emptied out. "I spoke with Claire the other day. I know someone I can call that might be able to help. He is familiar with these sorts of things," Gabriel said.

"Thank you, but I really don't think that's necessary. I mean, Claire is a little stir crazy. Her imagination kind of gets the best of her sometime. Honestly, there is nothing that we need help with. I appreciate your concerns but we're okay. It was a great service. We'll see you next week, Reverend," Jason shook the pastor's hand and quickly turned around, rolling his eyes and glaring at Claire.

Claire got into the car; eyes locked with Jason's. "That was rude."

"We don't need a house prayer, Claire! Or whatever that is,

we don't need it!" Jason snapped. "It's embarrassing for you to talk to everyone and blow this thing up. It's a small town and we don't want to be the talk of it. Again. Shit! A little nightmare and you think we need an exorcism! It's a dream! That's all. We all have them. That's part of sleep, now drop it!"

"What's gotten into you?" she snapped, turning her head away and wiping a tear from her face. "And unlock that fucking door upstairs!"

They sat in silence for a few minutes while Jason's mind wrestled with the past. The gossip and speculation surrounding the mysterious crash shifted in his thoughts. If there was one thing he couldn't take, it was becoming the new source of everyone's whispering tongues. Again. Small towns knew how to talk.

Claire was exasperated. "This isn't about your mother and the accident! It's about right here! Right now!"

Jason had succumbed to silence, and the car ride home was quiet, other than Sara in the back seat playing with her toys.

She bounced up and down in the seat, "Can we have pizza?"

"No!" Jason and Claire shouted at the same time, taking a quick angry glance at each other.

Claire took a deep breath, looking out the window, as Jason passed the dirt road with the bridge to take the long way home. "Jason, I get it. I do. But please listen to me. There is something."

"Not in front of Sara. Okay Claire, just... not in front of Sara."

They returned home and for the most part, the rest of the day was pretty quiet. Sara played upstairs with the pool table and Claire and Jason didn't have much to say to each other at all. Claire went into her darkroom and worked on developing the town pictures while Jason worked on grading papers for his class and kept an eye on Sara.

* * *

THERE WAS STILL VERY little conversation at dinner as they both picked at their food, lost in their own thoughts. After dinner, Claire took Sara upstairs and tucked her into bed. Before going downstairs, she walked over to the attic door and checked it. "Still closed and locked," she thought. "Maybe Jason's right, maybe I'm losing it." She hadn't thought about word maybe getting out until now. That was one of the biggest reasons they had moved from the town to start with. She crawled into bed and scooted next to Jason. "I'm sorry, you're right. I mean, it was a nightmare, granted a bad one. But still a nightmare that I let get in my head. It just really freaked me out and I suppose maybe the door wasn't shut all the way the first time. It hasn't opened since and... I'm sorry Jason. I don't know what I was thinking. I know your mom's accident in this town was a big thing with everyone. I wasn't thinking about that. It's just sometimes I think I'm going crazy here. I mean the thing with the pond and now all of this. I love you. I'm sorry. I won't say anything else about it, I promise. You can even leave that stupid door in the attic bolted for all I care. You're probably right. It's probably just attic space with more insulation."

"It's okay," Jason said, pulling her towards him. "To be honest, when we first moved into the house, I had a really scary dream myself, so I understand. I just don't want word getting around, and you know how this town is."

"You never told me that," Claire said. "I mean, about the dream. What was it?"

"No," Jason laughed. "I would really rather not repeat it and just let it go."

"Okay. I get it," Claire said. "I understand."

He held her in his arms tightly. "I love you. I'm sorry if I was snappy at church today."

"It's okay, no more boogie man or ghost talk," Claire laughed, reaching up to kiss him.

"Deal," Jason said, and they cuddled up together until they

fell asleep.

* * *

THAT NIGHT SARA was awakened by the sound of a dog barking outside. She started to think about the kitten and got out of bed. The house was dark and the floors creaked beneath her feet as she walked slowly down the steps towards the back door. Standing on her tip toes she reached up and was just tall enough to click the bolt and unlock the door. A gust of wind blew back her long blonde hair as she stepped out into the night.

"Kitty, kitty," she called out, looking around and walking past the pool. The porch light was fading out of sight the farther she walked. Her pink nightgown blew in the wind and a misty fog filled the dark night. She clung onto her doll tightly and called out again, "Kitty kitty kitty... come on kitty." A dog howled in the distance and she looked back at the house that seemed a million miles away through the thick fog.

A figure moved in the field and caught her eye. The dark shape of a woman with long hair waving in the wind began moving slowly towards her.

"Hey!" Sara called out. "Hello?" Sara held tightly to her doll, and the pit of her stomach began to feel sick. She glanced back toward the house nervously for a quick look, before locking her attention on the figure moving closer and closer towards her. She took a few steps backwards slowly, before a raven flew by her, letting out a loud raspy caw. She ducked down and shrieked in fear. Jerking around she ran as fast as she could back towards the house. Never looking back, she ran up the back porch, slammed the door and ran up the stairs to her room. Jumping into bed, she pulled the covers over her head, reaching out for a quick second to grab the little glass dragonfly. The barking faded in the distance as she gripped it tightly until eventually she fell asleep.

SOMETHING EVIL

*T*he next morning Jason went to work, and Claire
dropped Sara off at daycare.

Claire kissed Sara on the cheek as she squirmed out of the
car. "Bye pumpkin, love you."

"Bye Mommy, love you more," Sara said, and she ran into the
classroom, never saying a word about the night before. Claire
went back to the house and into her darkroom to finish developing the pictures. When she came to the pictures of the bookstore she stopped. "Maybe I'll drop in and visit Kristina today,
and eat some of those fantastic beignets she makes." She flipped
through the pictures until she came to the one she took of the
man outside the bookstore, the day she met Kristina. She looked
closely at the print but there seem to be a dark shadow of something next to him. She looked at another picture of the man but
the same shadow appeared on it also. She put the pictures
underneath her scope to see them better but she couldn't make
out what the dark shadow was. "Well these pictures are trash."
She threw them away thinking they must have been damaged
during developing. Gathering up the rest of the pictures, she
walked out of the darkroom and grabbed her purse to leave. Just

as she shut the front door behind her, the attic door creaked slowly open.

She drove into town and gave the pictures to the mayor. He was so happy with her work that he offered her another assignment, putting together a magazine on the town for visitors who passed through.

She had a couple of hours to kill and decided to go around town and shoot pictures of the locals enjoying some of the favorite spots on Main Street. When she arrived at the bookstore, she was excited to see Kristina and tell her the news.

"Kristina?" she called out as she stepped into the bookstore. "Hello?"

Kristina came out of the back with an older woman who was carrying a small black cloth sack.

"Just a minute Claire, I'll be right with you," Kristina smiled. She stepped aside with the woman and whispered something to her privately.

Claire felt a little awkward, so she did what she always did when she felt out of place.

"Smile," she said holding up the camera and taking a quick picture of the woman with Kristina. "Advertising for the bookstore," she said with an awkward look.

The woman glanced nervously at Kristina.

"It's alright, Mrs. Jimenez. I'll handle it," Kristina said, and she walked the woman out of the store.

Claire stood at the counter and when Kristina came back, she looked at her and smiled nervously.

"Sorry, I'm not sure why that made me so uncomfortable," Claire said. "When I'm nervous, taking pictures seems to calm me down."

Kristina walked over to Claire and gave her a stern look. "Claire, some of the things I help people with at the store, are private. Customers come in with special needs and they don't want anyone to know they come here. You understand?"

"Um, no," Claire said, shaking her head. "I mean, of course, but no harm ever came from books. Why would anyone care who comes here?"

Kristina laughed, "No, no harm ever came from books." She put her hand on Claire's arm and smiled. "No more pictures. What brings you out here today?"

"Um, I'm taking pictures for a travel magazine the mayor is putting in the local hotels. I thought I could maybe take some of you in front of the bookstore? Or just the bookstore if you would rather. I mean it would probably be good for business. If you want?"

"Of course," Kristina said. "Happy to help." She stepped behind the counter.

"Is now a good time?" Claire asked. She wanted to make sure Kristina was comfortable after the 'no more pictures' comment.

She raised her eyebrows and smiled at Claire. "Yes, now is fine. Would you like me to stand here or move somewhere else?"

"There is perfect." She started clicking pictures as she moved around to catch different angles. "So...what kind of special things do you help people with?"

"One day, I'll tell you all about it," Kristina said. "But not today, I have a customer coming in this afternoon that I must see."

She walked Claire to the door before ushering her outside and Claire turned quickly to take one last picture in front of store.

* * *

SHE PICKED up Sara and returned home. Sitting her camera in the darkroom, she grabbed a board game to play with Sara.

"Wait Mom, I want to get my doll," Sara said, and she ran up the stairs towards her bedroom.

"Okay, I'll get some cookies," Claire walked into the kitchen and got a white saucer down and put some cookies on it that she had baked the night before. She returned to the living room and set up the board game and began to eat one of the cookies. She looked up towards the stairs but didn't see or hear Sara.

"Sara! You get lost?" she called out. "I'm going to eat all these cookies," she laughed, taking another cookie off the tray.

She looked towards the stairs again but couldn't see Sara anywhere and the house was deadly silent.

"Sara?" she was a little concerned as she got up and started to walk towards the stairwell.

The wooden stairs creaked beneath her footsteps as she slowly walked up the stairs. "Sara?"

There was no response. Sara stood frozen, with her doll lying on the floor, staring at the open attic door. Claire gasped and grabbed Sara, jerking her close, her eyes locked on the open door. Her breathing quickened as she walked slowly backwards, away from the attic, holding onto Sara. She turned with a quick jerk, and ran down the stairs and into her bedroom, locking the bolt at the top of the door.

"Sara, watch cartoons. I need to call your dad." She picked up the phone, but the call went straight to his voicemail. "Jason, please call me! It's important."

Claire looked at Sara and took a deep breath. "Wait here."

"Mom, there was a..." Sara stopped and stared at Claire; her eyes filled with tears.

"Wait here," Claire said. "I'll be right back."

Claire went into the kitchen, frantically searching under the sink, she grabbed a hammer and started rummaging through the drawers. She grabbed three long nails under a stack of papers and headed slowly up the stairs. Reaching the top stair, she looked around the corner at the attic door that was still open wide. Quietly she crossed the room, pushing her fear deep down, she reached for the door and slammed it shut. Her hands trembled as she grabbed the nails, one by one, she slammed the hammer onto the nails until finally the door was nailed shut. The house returned to silence as she slumped on the floor exasperated, closing her eyes she took a deep breath. For a moment she sat, her back pressed against the leg of the pool table as she stared at the door. She felt a strange sense of peace. Getting up and heading back towards the stairs, she gave the door one last glance.

"Open that!" she said sarcastically, and walked back down the stairs.

The phone rang, it was Jason calling. "Claire, what's wrong? Are you okay?"

"I'm okay," Claire said. "The... I... had a situation here, but I handled it. Everything is okay."

"You had me worried. You sounded frantic on the phone. What happened?" he asked.

"Nothing really. I'll tell you later." She was in no mood to hear Jason's doubting response to what she was having to deal with in the house and after all, she had promised him no more.

Sara and Claire stayed downstairs in her bedroom with the door bolted shut until Jason returned home that evening. As they lay there on the bed watching television and waiting, Claire gazed up at the bolt on the bedroom door. It dawned on her for the first time: maybe Charlotte was trying to keep something in the house out of her room.

* * *

WHEN JASON RETURNED, he found Claire and Sara asleep in the locked bedroom. He knocked on the door. "Claire, is everything okay?"

Startled, she quickly got out of bed and hurried across the room, reaching up, she unlocked the door. "Jason, it was the attic door again." She flung her arms around his neck and buried her face into his chest, hugging him tight. "It was open." She mumbled, "I had to nail it shut! I was so scared."

"Claire, what's going on? What are you talking about?" He pushed her back, searching her face for an explanation. "What happened?"

"The attic door! Aren't you listening to me? It was locked! I went upstairs to get Sara and it was open. Wide open!" She ran her fingers through her hair, shaking her head.

"Claire, calm down. There has to be an explanation. You're being erratic." He pulled away from her and walked into the living room. "You're going to scare Sara if you don't stop fixating on that damn attic! You said you would stop all this."

"Okay Jason, you're right! There is an explanation! How about: there is something in that attic! You can't keep pretending like nothing is going on. What about the bolt on our bedroom door? What was Charlotte trying to keep out? The stomping above us night after night. You hear nothing? Nothing? I'm just crazy, right?!" Claire wiped the tears from her face and sat on the couch.

Jason took a deep breath and sat next to her. "So you nailed the door shut? You know Claire, air pressure in these old houses..."

"Open a locked door?!" Claire interrupted. "I think there is something in this house. Jason, please..."

Frustrated, he turned to her and chuckled sarcastically. "So you nailed it shut? Because a ghost, or whatever you think this is, can't go through a wall? Oh, I'm sorry, or apparently a bolted door either? Somehow, I don't think we have much to worry about if it's stopped by nails and bolts."

"Jason, please. Listen to me." She turned to him and put her hand softly on his arm. "Something is going on in this house. Maybe Charlotte knew about it and put the bolt on because she was scared."

"Look, I don't know how the door opened but I know my

grandmother. She lived alone. She put the bolt on in case anyone broke into the house, not to try and stop a ghost. You're letting your imagination run away with you. If bolts and nails work then it can't get any of us anyway." Exasperated, he got up and walked towards the bedroom. "I have to shower; it's been a long day, Claire." He grabbed his clothes from the dresser and walked into the bathroom with Claire close behind.

"It's easy for you to joke because you're not here. You don't deal with this thing every day."

"Claire! Stop it." He shoved her out of the bathroom and closed the door.

"Fine!" she screamed. "I hope that thing messes with you for once! Have a great fucking shower!" she looked over at Sara still sound asleep on the bed and stormed out of the room. Slamming the back door shut behind her, she walked outside and sat down on the ground, staring towards the field.

* * *

AFTER A WHILE, Jason stepped outside and sat down beside her. "Look, I'm sorry that you're going through whatever this is, it's just... I don't believe in stuff like that, and trust me, somewhere there is a logical explanation. I promise." He reached over and tried to give Claire a comforting hug but she pulled away.

"Jason, I'm telling you. I may not know what it is, but it's something." She turned away, staring back out at the field. She glanced at him and sighed. "There is something going on in this house and I need you to believe me."

"Okay," Jason said, taking a hold of her hand. "I'll tell you what, I'll send an air-conditioning guy out in the morning to look at the system and check everything out. Okay? I think you're going to see it's the pressure from the AC kicking on, and I'll even check the lock myself." He reached down and kissed Claire on the forehead. "If it makes you feel better, I'll have them check out the door inside the attic too. I'll cut the bolt off myself. Okay?"

"Okay," she agreed, but she looked less convinced than Jason had hoped.

They walked back into the house and Jason went upstairs to look at the attic door, which was still nailed shut. "She actually nailed it shut." He turned the knob anyway which felt pretty secure to him and then came back downstairs. It was getting late so he picked up Sara and took her upstairs and put her on her bed. He looked back at the attic door nailed shut while he started to walk downstairs. "Well, nothing is getting out of there," he said sarcastically, shaking his head, still in disbelief.

Claire crawled into bed, staring at the bedroom door. She turned on the television to help take her mind off of everything. She prayed silently to herself, "God, please protect me and Sara while we sleep, please, amen." She still felt angry that Jason wasn't taking anything she told him seriously. In some ways she wished something would show itself to him so that he would stop treating her like an irrational child.

Jason came back downstairs and crawled into bed. Neither of them had much to say as they watched the television, lost in their own thoughts, until eventually they fell asleep. The rain hit the house like thousands of tiny beads hitting a tin roof, and the wind howled through the trees.

JASON WOKE up startled to find Sara standing at the foot of their bed.

"Sara? What are doing out of bed?"

She didn't say anything but stood frozen, staring at him as if in a trance.

"Sara? Are you okay?" He got out of bed and moved closer towards her.

She looked at Jason, her eyes rolled back in her head and

became white. Her hair blew back as a gust of wind hit her face, and her mouth dropped wide open. Her lower jaw clicked loudly as it dislocated, and her chin dropped down to her chest. Her skin became wrinkled and she let out a terrifying groan.

JASON JERKED awake and looked around the room trying to catch his breath, his heart beating rapidly from the dream. Out of the corner of his eye he thought he saw a dark shadow move in the bathroom. Jerking his head towards the shadow, he jumped out of bed and turned the bathroom light on. He looked around, wiping the sweat from his forehead, but nothing was there. He looked over at Claire still sleeping. He could picture Sara in his mind, and decided to check on her. The rain poured heavily against the house as the storm grew stronger. He walked up the stairs to Sara's room and opened her door slowly. She was sleeping peacefully, clutching the dragonfly in one hand and her baby doll in the other. Closing the door, he started to walk back down the stairs when he heard a noise coming from one of the other rooms. Footsteps ran across the wooden floor in the bedroom farthest down the hall and the light downstairs flickered. Jason stood still for a moment, then slowly walked back up the stairs, his eyes fixed on the door at the end of the hall. He turned on the light in the hallway and moved closer to the room. Pounding footsteps ran across the floor again. He glanced at Sara's door and moved past the second bedroom, closer to the noise. As he reached for the doorknob, the hall light shut off. He turned around quickly and stared down the empty hallway, his hand still gripping the doorknob.

"Claire?" he called out nervously. Stepping back towards the hall light, he flipped the switch back on. His chest began to tighten and a chill filled his body. He stood in front of the bathroom, staring at the doorway at the end of the hall. A deep voice crept through the silence and whispered in his ear,

"Jason." Startled, he jerked around and a dark shadow figure stood against the wall in the game room. It rushed towards him and the lights in the house went off. Jason screamed and fell back into the bathroom, slamming the door shut. Heavy breathing came from the other side of the door and it groaned in a deep raspy voice, "Jason." The door started to shake and he pressed himself firmly against it. His eyes widened and he let out a loud desperate scream. Fingernails scraped down the other side of the door like claws ripping through the wood. Jason screamed out again, "Claire!" All of the sudden the sound stopped and the lights came on. Jerking the door open, he ran down the stairs, out the back door and fell upon his knees in the rain, trying to catch his breath. His heart was pounding so hard he thought it might pop out of his chest. As he held his face in his hands, trying to wrap his mind around what happened it dawned on him that he left Sara and Claire inside the house. He jumped to his feet. Sitting at the back door was the black dog, growling at him as if it were guarding the entrance. Jason froze, locking eyes with the dog. A sound came from behind him. He turned quickly, but all he could see were the trees blowing as the rain poured through the night. A voice called out from the house.

"Jason!" It was Claire, standing in the doorway. "What are you doing out here?"

Jason's eyes searched the yard, but the dog was nowhere in sight.

Jason screamed out, "Claire!" He was still in shock as he ran up and wrapped his arms around her, hugging her tight. "I'm sorry, Claire. I'm sorry I didn't believe you! We have to get out of here!"

"Sara!" He ran past her and upstairs where Sara was sleeping and opened her door. She was sound asleep when Jason picked her up and moved her downstairs to put her in bed with him and Claire.

"Until we figure this out, no one goes upstairs!" Jason said. "Something... Something is up there!"

"What happened to you? That's what I've been trying to tell you," Claire said.

"Let's just try and get some sleep..." He sat on the bed next to Sara.

Claire could see he was upset and couldn't help but feel a little guilty for the moment of slight happiness she got out of seeing him standing in the rain. "I'm sorry, I said I wished it would, you know, mess with you. I didn't know. I mean. I'm sorry."

"Me too," Jason said. He shook his head, "I'm sorry I didn't believe you. We all sleep together from now on. I'm not leaving Sara up there anymore."

Claire agreed and Jason shut and bolted their bedroom door. Claire turned on the television and after a while they fell asleep.

* * *

THE NEXT MORNING, they began to get ready for the day but Jason's mind was still focused on the night before. The rain had finally stopped, but water flooded the grounds outside. Claire went into the kitchen to fix breakfast, as Jason stared out of the window of their bedroom.

"Claire," Jason called out.

Claire stepped back into the room. "What is it?"

"I was thinking. We need to call Pastor Gabriel and see if he can help, or if he will at least come pray over the house. You know, maybe then whatever it is will go away and everything can go back to normal."

"I have some work to do in the darkroom but after that I can go into town and speak with him," she replied.

"No," Jason said. "I'll call in and take today off work, and go speak to him myself. That's the least I can do after I was short with him last week."

"Okay," she walked over and wrapped her arms around Jason's neck and held him close to her.

"I'll drop Sara off at the daycare," Jason said. "I don't want her here today while you're working in the darkroom."

"Okay, I love you." She squeezed him a bit tighter.

"I love you too, I'm sorry I didn't believe you. It's just I remember when I was little and my mom use to talk about things like this and I never believed her either. I thought she was just trying to make me stay inside or keep me from doing something she didn't want me to do. You know kind of using it to scare me into doing what she wanted. I never believed she was actually telling the truth. Claire, I've never told you this, but my mom... The night she died, she wanted me to go with her. She was afraid of something. I didn't believe her. Maybe if I had gone, she would still be here."

She held his hand. "No one knows what happened to your mom. You can't blame yourself. If you'd gone that night you wouldn't be here either. Those marks... Jason, no one knows."

AFTER BREAKFAST, Jason took Sara and dropped her off at the daycare and drove towards Sunnyside church to look for the pastor. As he drove past all the buildings to the church, he tried to rationalize in his mind what had happened the night before. "Could I have been sleepwalking? How could this be happening?" He parked the truck in the church parking lot and got out and walked up the hill, but when he tried to open the doors, he found them locked. He walked around the side of the church but the doors on the side were locked as well. He got back inside his truck and stared at the steering wheel. He felt numb and helpless as he tried to think of ways to protect his family. He was startled by someone knocking on his window.

"Good morning," Pastor Gabriel said with a big smile. "Are you looking for me?"

Jason smiled. Opening the truck door, he stepped out and closed it shut. "Yes," he was relieved to see him. "I need to speak with you. It's about the house, or rather something that is going on at the house." He felt a little embarrassed at his previous actions on Sunday.

"Step inside, son." Gabriel smiled and patted his hand on Jason's shoulder.

They walked into the church and into the back office. Jason sat down across from the pastor. "This is going to sound crazy and I wouldn't have believed it myself, except... it happened."

He told the pastor everything about the night before.

"I know you spoke to Claire, but I don't understand any of this. What can we do? I didn't know where else to turn." He looked down at his hands fidgeting nervously.

Gabriel sat back in his chair, looking down at the desk, then back at Jason, "Whatever is in that house, it's there for a reason."

"What do you mean?"

"There is something in that house that is drawing it. Something that let it in to start with. The stronger the evil is, the more power it has and the more dangerous it can become. We can pray over the house and God will drive it away, but if you don't find out what is causing its presence and destroy it, it will only return stronger than before. It has already shown itself to you. Things will only get worse from here if it isn't stopped." He reached in the cabinet behind his desk and pulled out a folder, "Jason, I didn't want to mention this to Claire before but the more you folks tell me the more this seems all too familiar to me. I seem to recall something like this happening in this town years ago. I was working with Father Taylor from the French Quarter. There was a girl, here in town, who was having all kinds of problems. Things attacking her when she slept, hounds following her and when she was awake it became worse. Gabby Peterson... I'll never forget it. One day she just left town and it all stopped. But right around the same time there was a deadly virus that broke out. Business closed down; people got sick. Had to stay home from work even. A lot of people died... it was the worst virus in history for our town. It was an awful thing." He paused and pulled a number out of the folder and looked at it and back at Jason, "I'll give Father Taylor a call. It's been a while since we spoke of such things, but back then he knew a lot more than he was willing to tell. Until then, look around the house, see if you notice anything unusual. They are drawn to certain things, certain places. All houses have their secrets. Often its weakness can be found in the same place as the root."

"How will I know what to look for?" He was even more puzzled than before. "And what do I do when I find it?"

"You will know when you see it. Trust God, He will show you what to do when the time is right," the pastor replied. "Have faith." He shook Jason's hand as he stood up. "I'll call Father Taylor this afternoon. Jason, these things have a way of becoming more active the more you take an interest in them so whatever you do, don't let it know what you're looking for."

Jason left the church and started to drive back towards the house. He didn't know if he actually felt any better or not. "How could this have happened before? The hound, is that what that dog is? Maybe we should just move. How am I supposed to know where to look or what to do?" He thought about every-thing that Gabriel had told him and the fact that he knew Tom Peterson well but had never heard anything about any of this from him. "Maybe I should speak to Tom. If they were able to get rid of it back then, maybe they'd know what to do."

He turned around and drove back to Main Street toward the red door hardware store. As he stepped out onto the sidewalk, he saw Tom heading in. "Tom," he called out.

Tom was surprised. "Jason! My God man, how have you been? I just seen Claire and that beautiful daughter of yours the other day. I'm so sorry about Charlotte. Come in, what can I help you with?"

Jason ran his fingers through his hair and took a quick look around the hardware store to see if anyone else was in there. "Tom, it's really good to see you. Actually, I wanted to come in and ask you about something."

"Sure, what is it?" he asked curiously.

Jason leaned over the counter and lowered his voice. "Whatever happened to your sister, Gabby?"

"Oh, Gabby?" Tom laughed loudly. "I thought you needed my help the way you were acting. She is doing great. She opened up a little incense shop over in the Quarters a long time ago. Why do you ask?"

Jason stood back up, searching Tom's face. "Why did she leave? I mean I heard that was around the same time the town had some major flu outbreak or something. Was she sick?"

Tom turned around and sat on a stool behind the counter looking at Jason. His bottom lip tightened up. "I was quite little at the time. To tell you the truth, I don't remember much. Why all the curiosity about Gabby and that flu outbreak?"

Jason tried not to look directly at Tom as he decided he wasn't going to get much information from him anyway. "Oh, just curious, nothing really. Claire is doing some research on the town, putting together a magazine for tourists, and came across a bit of information about the virus that broke out. I thought that would probably be around Gabby's teenage days. I wanted to see if there was any additional information that I could pass on to Claire. For the magazine."

Tom searched Jason's face for clues, then broke out into a laugh, "Jason, you always were funny! I wouldn't put the town's worst sickness in the travel magazine, inviting folks to stay here." He reached across the counter and gave Jason a bit of a bear hug. "I sure have missed that sense of humor around here."

Jason reluctantly took the overgrown bear hug and gave his best fake laugh back to Tom. "Yeah, just fooling around a bit." He laughed, "I just wanted to come in and say hello."

"Well hell man, stop in any time. Maybe we can go grab a beer sometime if you can get away from Claire for a while," he laughed.

Jason shook his hand. "Will do. I'll give you a call. I should probably get home. It was great seeing you again."

He left the store feeling a bit foolish and walked to his truck and got in to drive home. "That was pointless. Town magazine... stupid."

He drove back towards the house on autopilot as his mind drifted off to the night before. Before he knew it, he was on the dirt road in front of the bridge and he slammed on the brakes. His eyes blurred and for a moment it looked as if the bridge in front of him was moving.

He put the truck in reverse and slowly backed up, eyes straining to focus on the bridge.

"No, not a chance!" He turned the truck around and took the long way home.

THE MIRROR

*C*laire was in the darkroom developing the town pictures when she noticed something odd about one of the prints. The picture she took, of the woman standing with Kristina in the bookstore. It appeared to have a small dark shadow behind the woman holding the bag. Claire examined the image under her scope. She quickly rummaged through the trash, pulling out the picture of the man from before and compared the two. The dark shadows were identical. She scanned through the remaining pictures, looking carefully at each one. There it was! A picture she took of the ice cream shop next to the bookstore. If you look closely in the background, you could see there was a woman walking out of the bookstore carrying a small black bag. The dark shadow appeared next to the woman in this picture as well. Claire's eyes widened as she looked up from the table. She went through the stack of pictures until she found the one she took of Kristina but much to her surprise, there were no dark shadows. She started to look through the pictures she took of Sara that day at the pond and shuffled through them quickly until she came to the pictures of the wind chimes on the shack and the symbols on the wooden door frame. She held the pictures in her hand and headed out of the darkroom.

Walking back into the kitchen, she poured herself a cup of tea. She flicked through the images in her mind, trying to make sense of them: the dark shadow, the symbols on the doorframe. She decided to see if she could find them anywhere on the internet, but as she scrolled through several symbols none of them resembled the signs she was looking for. She remembered what Kristina had told her, that they could be for harvesting or something like that. She looked up symbols for harvesting and finally she came across one that resembled one of the markings. It was a sign that meant rebirth or resurrection, which made no sense to her, and only confused things more. She felt exhausted and lay back on the couch, setting the pictures on the coffee table, closing her laptop and looking up at the ceiling thinking, until after a while she fell asleep.

A dark shadow figure moved slowly through the house and loomed over Claire as she lay asleep. It tilted its head back, dropping its mouth wide open and let out an eerie scream as it crawled on top of her. Claire's breathing quickened as its whispers flooded the air. She began to dream.

SHE OPENED HER EYES, *still lying on the couch. She struggled to sit up but was paralyzed. Gasping for air, she tried to breathe but something heavy was on top of her chest. "What's happening?" She began to panic as she looked around the room. The television was on the same channel and her cup of tea sat on the coffee table next to her. She couldn't see anything on top of her but she could feel the weight of it and the presence of evil surrounded her. She felt sickened by the feel of it and no matter how much she struggled her body was unable to move.*

It slid its hand over her mouth and whispered, "No one can help you."

Gasping for air, she tried to scream but nothing came out. She could see her clothes being ripped off her body as her eyes widened and frantically darted around the room, until she saw the image in the mirror on the wall, and her eyes locked on it in disbelief. The pressure on top of her grew heavier. She fixated on the image in the mirror that appeared to be lying on top of her. It pressed its body firmly onto hers. Tears ran down her cheeks and she let out a terrified scream. She stared at the thing on top of her in the mirror. "No!" she cried out, but it only became stronger. Its face appeared distorted with rotten flesh, as something black dripped out of its mouth and landed on Claire's face. Her small body looked like a child's underneath the presence of the demon which covered her completely. Its webbed feet hung way past her own, and it had elongated arms which ran almost the length of her body. It slowly moved its hand up her leg and slid its pointy fingers between her thighs. The other hand pressed firmly across her mouth as she struggled to scream. She darted her eyes on her body but could see nothing and quickly looked back towards the mirror at the beast.

"Do you want to see me, Claire?" it whispered in a thousand voices.

Her body trembled and she tried to scream again but this time nothing came out. She felt helpless under its control. The demon slid its hand off of her mouth and Claire could feel its fingernail slide across her bottom lip, slicing it open as it ran its hand down her body and back up to her throat. It wrapped its fingers tightly around her neck as it began to squeeze. Its grip became tighter and tighter as she fought for air to breathe. The thick black liquid dripped out of the thing's mouth and onto her lips. Her eyes shifted back looking on top of her but she could see nothing; her body lay covered with sweat, helpless under the demon. She looked back in the mirror, and its eyes narrowed as it gazed at her with an evil grin. Its other hand pressed firmly between her legs. She could feel something sharp penetrating her over and over.

Closing her eyes tightly she gathered all the energy she had left and let out a final cry for help. "God Please! Help me! Jesus!"

HER EYES JERKED OPEN WIDE as she gasped for air and jumped off the couch. Tears poured down her face, her body covered in sweat, as she looked around the room frantically searching for the creature. She locked her eyes onto the mirror but there was nothing there. She was awake. The demon was nowhere to be seen. She shoveled her hands through the clothes on her body to reassure herself that she was still dressed as she let out a loud frantic scream that echoed through the house. Her body shook as she walked slowly over to the mirror and lifted her hair to examine what felt like a burning on her neck. Four red marks stretched across her throat. She ran her hands down her thighs, checking her body. She could still feel a throbbing pain between her legs and she fell to the floor crying. It was a few minutes before she could bring herself to pick up the phone.

JASON STOPPED at the park near town and was sitting on the bench trying to think things through when he received the hysterical call from Claire.

"Shit! I shouldn't have left you there! I'm on my way."

He wanted to get there as fast as possible and decided to take the bridge. It was the quickest way to the house and Claire needed him. As soon as he came to the bridge, he stopped the truck and stared forward. The water rushed underneath the old bridge and he began to sweat as he started to drive the truck slowly across. He tried to focus his mind on Claire but the crash found its way back to the front of his thoughts. His mother's screams echoed in the wind and his breathing became shallow as his chest began to tighten up.

"I've got to get to Claire."

He kept pushing the gas, but it seemed to take forever to cross the bridge and he began to feel faint. He reached up, wiping the sweat from his brow, and glanced at the road behind him. He was closer to crossing than turning back, he would have to keep going. The screams became louder until the inside of his head felt like it was going to burst. Out of the corner of his eye he saw a dark figure standing on the side of the bridge. Startled he jerked the wheel to keep from hitting it and yelled out, "Nope! Not today!" He pressed the gas to the floor and plowed across the bridge at full speed. He felt a weird sense of freedom as he reached the other side and he burst into laughter as he yelled out, "Yes! Woo hoo! Yeah!" For a moment, everything else seem to disappear as he left the past in the review mirror, and the bridge far behind him. He was finally able to let it go, for Claire.

* * *

JASON REACHED the house and ran in the front door to find Claire still sitting on the floor in tears. He rushed over to her and she cried as he held her tightly. "It was so horrible, Jason. It was so real. I have marks on my throat." She pointed to the red streaks on her neck.

"I'm sorry, Claire." He shook his head and took her hand. "Listen, let's just move and get away from this place. We can go right now. We can send movers, packers, whatever, doesn't matter. Let's just go."

She took a deep breath, wiping the tears from her eyes. "Jason, whatever is happening here... I think it tried to kill me. What if it follows us or hurts Sara?" She picked up the pictures on the coffee table and handed them to Jason. "I found these symbols carved into the door on the shed by the pond and then I saw the same ones on a door in the back of the hardware store.

Maybe they mean something. I didn't want to say anything before but maybe we should show this to Gabriel and maybe he will know something. Maybe it's nothing, but it's worth a try."

"Did you say the hardware store?" He stared at her curiously.

"Yes, I mean I know it sounds stupid, but Jason, I'm grasping."

"Did you look in the shack?" He walked towards the back door and looked out the window.

"No, it was locked and then I was looking for Sara. It was the day that the thing with the pond happened and I forgot all about it until I was in the hardware store. I mean it may be nothing. I asked one of the other shop owners in town and they said it's probably just harvest signs, like to draw good luck. I don't know. I could only find one that even looked like one of the symbols online and it was something about rebirth. I don't know about anything anymore." She took a sip of her tea and sat back on the couch.

"I don't know either but it seems like creepy symbols on doors is a good place to start looking. I suggest we try and find the key to that shed. I spoke to Gabriel today. He has a friend that might know something about all of this. The guy is a priest." He glanced towards the stairs remembering Gabriel's advice not to talk about it in the house.

"What? A priest? How does he know about any of this? What are you talking about?" She looked at Jason, searching for answers. "We need to go show these things to Gabriel now."

"I don't know Claire. His friend is a priest, and I think he dealt with something like this before. I wasn't even going to bring it up," Jason said, leaning on the backdoor.

"What? Why?" She walked over and put her hand on Jason's shoulder. "We have to stop this."

"I know. Look, Gabriel already said he would call the guy and now, with what happened today..." He pulled Claire close to him.

"Jason, we need to tell Gabriel about the symbols. Besides we have to go pick up Sara anyway. Please, let's just go now. I'll feel like we at least did something," she pleaded.

He could tell she was still shaken and if anything, she probably needed out of the house for a while. "Okay Claire, grab your things. Let's go." He picked up his keys and walked towards the front door. As they both got into the car, Claire leaned over and kissed Jason on the cheek. "Thank you," she said, and smiled.

"For what?"

"For letting me get out of there. I know it was a dream but... it was so real." She covered the markings on her neck with her hand. "And why?"

"I'm just sorry I wasn't there sooner." He reached over and kissed her.

The drive was quiet as they drove back into town up to the church. Both of them rethinking their own theories of whatever was haunting their house. As they pulled into the church parking lot, Pastor Gabriel was just getting into his car to leave.

"Gabriel!" Claire shouted as she quickly got out of the car and ran over to him.

"Claire, I almost didn't see you," He looked surprised as he stepping back out of his car. "Jason, I feel like I just saw you today," he chuckled as he shut the car door and reached out to shake Jason's hand.

"Yeah, I'm sorry to bug you again, Pastor, but we had another incident at the house and I think we're probably grasping at straws but..." Jason was interrupted by Claire, who had laid the pictures on the hood of Gabriel's car.

"I found these symbols carved on the door of the shack out by our pond. Do they mean anything to you?" She searched Gabriel's face for clues.

He picked the pictures up and looked through them carefully. "There is something familiar about these markings." He looked at them closely again. "Let's go into my office for a moment I think I have something that can help." They walked back into the church and went in his office. Claire felt a little relief at the possibility of any kind of answers. Gabriel thumbed through some old books that were on a shelf until finally he found the book he was looking for. He sat back in his chair looking at the pictures and then opened the book and turned to a chapter. There was a picture of the symbols Claire had been searching for all morning. As Gabriel turned the book around, he pointed out each one that he could identify. "This symbol is a representation of something coming or a resurrection of some kind."

"Yes!" Claire said anxiously. "I found that one online. It said it meant rebirth or something."

"And this one represents a form of plague, or something evil being let loose." He pointed to the next symbol. "This one, I'm not sure, but this other one stands for pact with the beast."

"What?" Jason looked up at the pastor. "What does all that mean? Is this what you were saying we needed to look for? So, we get rid of the symbols and we get rid of that... thing? Who carved them?"

Gabriel closed the book and took the pictures. "I don't understand what all of this means myself, but we will find out."

Claire let out a sigh of relief. "I don't know how much longer I can take this, and I'm even more confused now."

Jason pulled her to him and hugged her tight. "It's going to be okay, I promise. Right, Gabriel?" He glanced back at the pastor for reassurance.

"Listen, I'm no expert at this sort of thing but like I told you earlier, I have a friend of mine in the French Quarter, Father Taylor, who is a real polymath." Gabriel tried to give Claire a comforting look. "I spoke to him earlier, but I wanted to talk to him about all of this in person. I was just headed that way to pick up some other things for the church and meet up with him for dinner. Claire, if you don't mind, I would like take these pictures with me and show them to him. I'm sure he will have more answers."

"Thank you! Thank you so much," Claire said, shaking her head and wiping another tear from her cheek.

"Pastor, I don't know how to thank you," Jason said, shaking Gabriel's hand.

"Don't thank me yet. I haven't helped you folks much." He smiled at them and got up from his chair. "I'll let you know what I find out, until then you folks be careful."

Jason and Claire walked outside and over to their car. They got in and looked at each other for a moment before anyone spoke.

"A pact with the beast? Like the devil? I can't believe any of this is happening." Jason shook his head and took a deep breath. "My grandmother couldn't have known about this. She wouldn't be able to carve these things. Claire, maybe someone was coming onto her property and she didn't even know it. And the hardware store? What does any of this even mean?"

Claire put her hand on Jason's leg, "I don't know, but hopefully Father Taylor will have more answers. So far, I don't like anything about those symbols. I say we go scratch them off!"

"No!" Jason said. "No one goes near that shed. If there is someone else involved, they could be watching us. You said you feel like someone is watching you while you're outside. So no one goes back there until we have more answers. Until then I think if we're still looking for answers, the attic is a good place to start."

"Okay," Claire took a deep breath and stared out the car window. "But I'm not comfortable knowing those symbol things are outside our house." She glanced down at her watch. "Jason, it's time to get Sara."

They drove to daycare to pick her up, and decided not to talk about any of it in front of her. They wanted to keep as much of it from her as possible. She was at the age that she listened way too closely to grown-up conversations, and they didn't want to scare her. For the most part whatever was in the house was leaving her alone. As she came out of daycare, she hopped into the back seat of the car and filled it with chatter from the events of the day.

"Let's go for pizza while we're in town," Jason said looking in the backseat at Sara. "Stay away from the house awhile," he whispered to Claire as he reached out and grabbed her hand and held it in his.

"I think that's a great idea," Claire replied. She was in no hurry to go anywhere near the house.

"Yeah! Pizza!" Sara said bouncing up and down in the backseat of the car.

The pizza parlor was always a good change of scenery and with Sara talking non-stop about life at daycare, for the moment, the house drifted far from Jason and Claire's mind.

That evening after they returned home Jason suggested they put a movie on in their room and watch it together. They all curled up in their bed and for the most part the house was quiet for the night.

It was early in the morning hours when Jason was awakened by a dog barking outside. He got out of bed, walked slowly towards the window and took a deep breath as he pulled back the curtain and looked out into the backyard. Much to his surprise he saw nothing but a clear night. He let out a sigh of relief and then stared at the pool in the backyard. Tiny white lights surrounded the grounds around the pool area. The water was a gorgeous color of blue from the inside pool light. It was almost hypnotic to look at under the stars at night. He thought about all the times he went night swimming when he was younger and how relaxing and beautiful it was. He thought about Charlotte and his mom and swimming under the stars at night. He missed them both very much. The accident was always with him and the guilt of not going with her that night. The feeling like maybe if he would have been there it wouldn't have happened. He stared at the pool and thought about it all.

He had just finished up college at the time of Cindy's death and no one could ever say what actually happened that night on Old River Road. The story was that, she worked late, probably fell asleep driving home, and ran off the bridge and into the bayou. The problem with the story was, when they pulled her car out, there were deep claw marks all over it, like an animal had ripped into it, but no animal could have done the damage that was done to that car and as for Cindy, well, it was a closed casket and the police never said anything else about it. The town filled up with stories of what people thought had happened. In a small town it's hard to hide facts from gossiping tongues and there was no shortage of those. Everywhere Jason went people were staring and whispering and talking about it for months. Jason was heartbroken and he and Claire left town as soon as they could, to escape the questioning minds of everyone around them. He had never been able to cross that bridge until now. Somehow facing the bridge helped bring him some closure but he still would have given anything to go back in time and go with her that night. He would never know what really happened, no one would.

Staring into the night, he wondered what it was like for his mom to raise him by herself. Working all those nights overtime just to make ends meet. Jason looked back at Claire and Sara sleeping peaceful in the bed and decided to go for a swim. He grabbed his swim trunks, stepped into the bathroom, changed, grabbed a towel and quietly went outside. The night air smelled clean and you could see every star in the sky and hear every sound playing in the bayou. It made him think of Charlotte and he ran and jumped in the pool. When he came up for air, he laughed a little. He swam laps in the pool and then floated on his back, staring up at the sky. The bayou was so peaceful floating there under the stars. He was out there for a while before he thought he saw something dark move from behind one of the trees which frightened him a little. Suddenly he remembered everything they were facing in the house and calmly he swam over to the side of the pool. He saw the shadow move beyond the trees again and remembered what Gabriel had said. "Pay them no attention. Don't let them notice you noticing them." He acted like he didn't see anything and pulled himself up out of the water. He grabbed his towel and walked towards the back door. In the distance a dog started to bark and as he glanced back locking in on the dark shadow moving closer toward him. He turned around quickly, as a chill shot through him, and he walked a little faster towards the house. He let out a sigh as he stepped inside, locked the door, and took one last look out of the window. There was nothing there. He took a deep breath and went into his bedroom where Claire and Sara were still sound asleep. He showered, put his pajamas back on and crawled back into bed. It was about four in the morning and he was exhausted. Finally, he was able to fall asleep.

A dark figure moved through the quiet house. The kitchen cabinets opened one by one as it moved through the rooms. The mirror in the living room fell off of the wall and broke on the floor as a book dropped from one of the shelves. The shadow creature moved into Jason and Claire's room and stood next to their bed. It tilted its head back and its mouth elongated as it arched its back and groaned. The blinds blew up on the window and the demon moved towards Jason, looming over him. Thousands of whispers flooded the air.

JASON GASPED *a quick breath and opened his eyes but was paralyzed from fear. He could feel someone or something's hand covering the side of his head and face as it pushed him down hard into the pillow. He knew he was dreaming but he couldn't wake*

up. The wind was blowing in the room all around him and Sara
was standing next to him on the side of the bed. He wanted to call
out to her but he couldn't. Her eyes were a hollow circle of burning
fire and her long blonde hair was blowing from the wind. Evil
filled the room around him as the hand pressed harder on the side
of his face. Each finger pressing down, burning through his skin as
it melted his flesh. He tried to scream but nothing would come out,
he could barely breathe. He remembered what Claire had done and
quickly said to himself, "God save me!" but an evil voice whispered
back at him, "Do you really think, you, are worth saving?" Then it
took its other hand and pressed its nails into Jason's chest and
clawed what felt like fire marks into his skin.

JASON WOKE up and screamed out for Claire. Startled she woke
up and barely caught a glimpse of the shadow leaving the room.

"Jason! Are you okay?" Claire reached for his arm.

He jumped out of bed and pulled up his shirt. His skin was
still burning and there were four red claw marks across his
chest just deep enough to draw blood.

"Oh my God!" exclaimed Claire, as she jumped out of bed.

They went into the bathroom to try and keep it from Sara
who was still managing to sleep through everything.

"What happened? What did this?" Her voice trembled as she
grabbed a washcloth and gently started wiping Jason's chest.

"That thing! Something burned me, clawed me! I don't
know!" Jason said, his voice was still shaking from the burning
pain in his chest. "This has to stop, Claire. What is it? What does
it want?"

"I don't know. Let me help you." She reached for the medi-
cine out of the cabinet.

"I was having such a great night, for once," Jason said, taking
a deep breath and closing his eyes. "For once... all of this was
gone."

As they got dressed, they went into the kitchen to sit down and drink a cup of coffee when they noticed all the cabinets open and the mirror broken on the floor. They both stopped, looked at each other and started to pick up the pieces of the mirror.

"I'll go into town today," Claire said as she walked in the kitchen and began to shut the cabinet doors. "Maybe there is a book or something at the bookstore that can help. Maybe Gabriel will find out something more and hopefully, Father Taylor will have answers... something has to give. We just have to hold on."

"My grandmother was as innocent as they come. I can't imagine that she would know anything about those symbols or any of this," Jason took another sip of coffee.

"Jason," Claire, turned around and put her hand on his shoulder. "Charlotte died in her sleep... in her sleep Jason. She had a bolt put on her bedroom door. What if she put it on her door to try and keep something out? What if? What if that thing was already here and had something to do with her death?"

"That's crazy," Jason said setting down his cup, "We're getting ahead of ourselves."

"It's all crazy! How do we know?" Claire pushed her hair back and walked over to the sink, "I mean... we don't even know what any of this is or how to deal with it. So we shouldn't sleep?" she slammed the last cabinet door shut and sat back down at the kitchen table.

"I don't know. Is there is a 1-800 Get That Demon out of Your House number?" Jason said sarcastically, trying to make her laugh a little and maybe put her at ease.

"No... I know... It's just frustrating and I'm scared," she took a deep breath and looked back at Jason.

"Hey... We're going to be okay, I promise," he put his hand on her cheek.

"I'm just..." she shook her head exasperated and got up. "I'm going to get my camera out of the darkroom."

She always found peace of mind in her camera and at the moment she needed some peace. As she stood in the darkroom, she started to look through the pictures again. She looked at the pictures of the people around the bookstore. "What is that shadow?" It was apparent that the shadow was not simply an error in developing but rather something dark in the pictures themselves. The man holding the black bag, the bookstore, Kristina, Mrs. Jimenez, the shadow was always present. The picture of the people in the background of the ice cream shop, holding the bookstore bag... the shadow just behind the woman with the black bag. "What the hell are in those bags?" She looked at the pictures of Kristina and the bookstore but there were no shadows or smudges. She thought about the dark figure she had caught glimpses of around the house and decided to talk to Kristina. She wanted to find out if Charlotte had said anything to her before she died and what work Charlotte actually did at the store. More importantly, she wanted to know what Kristina sold out of the back and what was in those black bags. She wasn't sure if there was a connection but she felt it was something worth looking into and she didn't want to stay at the house.

They finished their coffee and woke Sara to feed her breakfast and get her ready for the day. No one wanted to go back to sleep. They headed into town and the only talking was Sara going on and on about daycare. They were supposed to paint today and she was excited. It was actually a welcoming distraction that they were beginning to look forward to; a sense of normalcy amongst the madness. Claire didn't say anything to Jason about the bookstore or the shadows in the pictures. She knew how upset he was at the thought of Charlotte being killed in her sleep, and with everything he went through with his mother's death and the nightmare before, she thought it was best she kept this part to herself. They dropped off Sara, and Claire dropped Jason off at work.

"Be careful today," Jason said as he stepped out of the car. "Stay away from the house if you can and if you can't, then come pick me up and I'll go with you. I can get a substitute if I need one. Just don't go back there by yourself, okay?"

"Okay." She leaned over and kissed him goodbye. "I'm just going to try and work in town. I'll pick you up after lunch."

"See you soon. I love you and call me if you need me for anything," Jason said as he closed the door and headed into the school building.

Claire couldn't wait to get to the bookstore and see Kristina. She had so many questions that were running through her mind and she was desperately looking forward to hearing back from Gabriel and Father Taylor. "Maybe they had answers by now and the worst was behind them." She pulled into the parking lot at the end of Main Street, stepped out of the car and headed towards the bookstore.

THE HELL WITCH

*K*ristina Graves grew up inside the French Quarter in New Orleans, Louisiana. Her mother was a fortune teller on Bourbon Street and Kristina was taught the craft early on to help raise money for her family. Her grandmother was considered one of New Orleans most powerful voodoo priestesses. She was originally from Togo in Africa, and came from a long line of people that practiced the religion of voodoo.

There were always strange things happening around Kristina when she was growing up. People came from miles away to see her grandmother or her mother. They wanted seances to talk to a loved one that had passed away or to have their fortune read. Some came to get potions to help them win the heart of someone they loved or to seek revenge on others they despised. Witchery was a normal everyday conversation and so were the things that came to move around late in the night.

She was six years old the first time she heard what she would later discover was the Hell Witch, in her house. It was late one night when she was home alone, asleep in her bed, and the sound in the hallway woke her up. In those days, she was often left alone after dark while her mother worked on the street outside of their townhouse. She had a table set up and read fortunes for people that passed by, partying through the night. New Orleans was one of those cities that never slept and the French Quarter had a long history of vibrant parades and drinking party goers who filled the streets.

That night was hot and humid. The floors creaked under heavy footsteps as they moved slowly towards her room. "Mom, is that you?" She sat up in bed and listened intently. Heavy breathing filled the hallway outside of her room. She grabbed her teddy bear and pulled the covers over her head to try and hide herself from the sound as it drew closer to her room. Her breathing quickened and she tried to hold her tears back so as not to make a sound, as the squeaky bedroom door slowly opened. The heavy breathing moved closer to her bedside and she squeezed her eyes shut. She remembered the purple talisman her grandmother had given her to protect her from evil spirits. She kept it under her pillow at all times. Icy smoke came out of her mouth in short breaths as a cold chill filled the air. Kristina reached under her pillow and grabbed the talisman. As she clenched it in her hand, she began to chant a spell she had learned from her grandmother to ward off evil spirits. Within a few moments, the sound disappeared. She waited a few minutes and peered out from the covers to take a look around the room. It was gone. She wiped her hand across her face and lay back down holding her teddy bear tightly until she fell asleep. Unfortunately, this would be only the beginning, for the Hell Witch came to torment Kristina many times throughout her life, and each time she returned even stronger than before. Kristina told no one about the visits, except a young priest who worked with the kids in town, Father Taylor of St. Anne's catholic church. He seemed to listen and take her seriously, and he taught her new ways to fight the witch off.

Crosses that were dipped in holy water seemed to work best, and despite the fact that he tried to steer her away from it, Kristina soon became quite the voodoo priestess herself.

When she was ten, she was awakened one night by a pack of black dogs that were howling beneath her window, scratching and clawing their way up to the building. When she looked out beyond the dogs, she could see in the street-lights a black figure of a woman standing, staring at her. She could see no face, just black, vacant darkness, with long flowing hair and icy blue eyes. She could see the shadow of a long dress billowing in the night wind, and as the witch opened its mouth it let out a loud groan directed towards Kristina.

Her entire body tensed up as she jerked the curtains closed and jumped back away from the window. She ran to her closet, grabbed a box off the top shelf and sat down on the floor with the box in front of her. As she opened the wooden box, heavy breathing echoed throughout her room and Kristina froze. She tried to hold her breath to be as quiet as she could as she rummaged through the box. The pounding of footsteps crossed slowly across her bedroom towards the closet and she knew it was the Hell Witch returned. "I have to move; I have to stop it." She frantically searched the inside of the box but as she started to move the footsteps stopped closely behind her. A hot airy breath blew on the back of her neck. Terrified, she froze. The wooden floor became frigid beneath her, as a cold air swept across the room. In a thousand voices, it whispered in her ear, "Kristina, it's coming."

Her breathing became shallow and every part of her body tensed up with fear as she began to shake. Forcing her hands to move she pulled three talismans from the box and put them on the floor in front of her, the purple talisman centered between the other two stones. She closed her eyes, laid her hands across them and began to chant. The sound of the breathing soon stopped and the cold seemed to dissipate out of the air around her. She gasped as her eyes darted across every inch of the room. The Hell Witch had disappeared along with the black dogs, and she let out a deep sigh of relief. She put the talismans back in the box along with a mixture of amulets and charms and placed her favorite teddy bear with blue button eyes on top and sat the box back on the shelf.

* * *

As time went by Kristina learned many things growing up in the quarter. She had inherited her family's gift of the craft and perfected reading tarot cards. She soon became quite skilled at all the things that tourist wanted when they came through town; money potions, lucky talismans, love potions and tales of what their future would hold. She worked part time on the weekends to help raise money for the family and on good nights her mother let her keep some of the tips for herself.

Late at night, after the tourists were long gone, there was a very different side of the craft... a side that was only for a select few of the locals to see. When Kristina turned sixteen, she was taught that also. It was what made the difference between a street teller and a true voodoo priestess. One told stories of what people wanted to hear, while the other actually had the gift of sight, and knew the craft. She had always had the gift or the curse, depending on how you looked at it. They say you were chosen way before you were born and that your path would lead you directly into the cult and so for Kristina the stories were true.

* * *

It was October 15th, 1981, when Kristina turned sixteen years of age. She was excited about the day and had been antici-pating it for weeks. She had big plans of going out with her friends and walking the night streets and maybe even getting her first kiss from David Stoneking. He was a boy she had gone to school with since the fourth grade. All the girls at school had a crush on him. He had dark hair and mesmerizing brown eyes with long lashes. They had always been friends but that night she was hoping to take it to the next level and steal a birthday kiss.

As she rushed through the day giggling with her friends, they set up their time to meet that night. When Kristina returned home, she spent some time with her family, constantly checking her watch. Her mom agreed she could have her time between ten and one with her friends on the street. It was her rite of passage, turning sixteen in the Quarter. The time came, and out the door she ran to meet up with her friends.

There was a group of about ten of them including David. They went up and down the streets drinking, laughing and pointing out the drunk people dancing in the streets. In the Quarter if you were underage no one noticed you drinking as long as you were discreet. They walked around the side of one of the buildings and Kristina's wish came true, David reached over and gave her a birthday kiss. It was a perfect night and for a moment, Kristina was just a normal sixteen-year-old girl, getting a kiss from a boy she thought to be her true love, on her birthday. As one o'clock rolled around, Kristina said goodbye to her friends and headed home. Before leaving David reached out and gave her another kiss and brushed his hand across her cheek, "We'll always be together Kristina, always." He gave her a quick wink and left with their friends, and she walked up the steps of her house, as if in a love-sick daze.

The streets had become vacant, and as the wind blew the night air seemed to get colder all at once. She walked in the door and her mother and her aunt were sitting at the table waiting for her.

"Come child," her mother said, getting up from the table. "It's time."

"Time for what?" Kristina asked, still a little buzzed from the night.

"Time for you to learn the secrets of the craft," her mother replied, and she took Kristina's hand and walked her out the back door and towards the woods behind the house.

For a minute, Kristina thought they must be playing a trick on her, but their faces were expressionless. She knew her mother well and when she had that look, she wasn't playing around.

She gave Kristina a black robe and told her to put it on. When they reached deep into the woods, there were a group of people with robes on, standing in a circle, waiting for them. Their faces were covered with masks, so Kristina could not see who they were. They had a big fire burning in the middle of the circle and a man was standing at the front with his face painted white and black, and he was reciting a chant that Kristina had never heard. She began to get a little nervous. If there was one thing she had learned early on from her grandmother, it was that chanting with the proper elements could bring about powerful sorcery, and she wasn't sure what they were saying or what they were trying to bring about. The night air continued to get colder, and Kristina's mother and aunt joined in the circle and began the chant, as the wind picked up and the fire rode higher, Kristina stood nervously in front. Out of the trees, a fog rolled in from off the bayou, and became thick all around them. So thick that if it wasn't for the light from the fire, Kristina wouldn't have been able to see anyone at all. Crows filled the night sky, and hundreds of harsh caws flooded the air.

She heard a noise from the darkness, beyond the trees and when she looked over, she thought she saw something step out of the woods coming towards them. It had a body of a man but the head of a bull. She blinked her eyes a couple of times to make sure she was seeing what she thought. She watched as, step by step, it moved closer. Her eyes widened as she fixated on it and gasped to catch her breath. It had big black horns that came out of its head and red fiery eyes. It was huge, and had what looked like hooves instead of feet, and hair that covered its body. Kristina wanted to scream but she couldn't speak and the chanting became even louder. Not only was it around her but it echoed inside of her head and began to take over her own thoughts. Her mother leaned over and whispered, "Kristina, open your mouth." She wasn't sure why she did it, but she did, even though she couldn't take her eyes off the thing that now stood directly in front of her. She was frozen with fear, standing in front of this beast, looking up at it with her mouth wide open.

It had fingers like a man but long claw-like nails and it had something in its hand that it shoved into Kristina's mouth. It was thick like mucus and Kristina thought she was going to throw up. Her stomach was immediately sick and her body felt like she could fall to the ground at any minute. The substance filled her mouth so much that it ran down her chin and she gagged a little not knowing if she should try and swallow it or not. The beast was hypnotic staring through her and she could not take her eyes away from it. She felt dizzy and it took its hand and put it on top of her head and pushed her to the ground on her knees in front of it. She tried to look up but it dug its claws into her head and pushed her head back downward again. She felt sick and dizzy and out of the corner of her eye she could see someone else had been brought into the circle, someone new. She tried to look and see who it was but the beast held her head steady so she could look nowhere but down. The chanting and the sound of crows echoed loudly and the fire burned high; the fog was thick and the wind blew cold through the night as the group of people circled around Kristina who was knelt beneath the beast. Her eyes filled with tears and everything became blurred.

"Please! NO!" She heard a male voice scream out, a voice she thought she recognized, but it was quickly muffled. She tried to look up again but the beast grabbed her face and she could feel the piercing of its nails go through her skin. Once again, her mother whispered in her ear, "Open your mouth," as she grabbed hold of Kristina and pulled her up to her feet. She didn't want to do it, but the beast squeezed her face harder and dug its nails into her skin until her mouth dropped open. Tears burned like fire as they ran down her cheeks and once again the black, thick mucus substance was shoved in her mouth by the hairy palm of the beast. It forced her back to her knees, and this time Kristina threw up on the ground. She wanted to collapse but the beast held firmly onto her hair, keeping her from falling to the ground. In the midst of the chanting she heard a voice that sounded like rushing water whisper to her, "You will release the fifth demon then you will always be mine." Someone shoved a cup into her hand filled with a thick red substance and forced it to her mouth. "Drink, child!" The stench was strong and her stomach weakened. She wasn't sure how much more she could take when everything faded to black and the chanting stopped. She collapsed on the ground and slowly opened her eyes, pushing herself up just enough to turn her head towards the fire. She caught a glimpse of the dark figure she had seen before, with long hair and piercing blue eyes, standing just beyond the circle. The woods took on a deafening silence and out of the smoke arose a huge shadow creature with elongate arms that hung down past its knees. Her eyes widened and she struggled to breathe as it began to come into focus. It had long fingers with sharp tarnished nails and red hallow eyes. It tilted its head up and looked at the sky as it held out its arms and screamed a low pitch groan of a thousand voices that pierced Kristina's ears. Black smoke came pouring out of its mouth and dissipated into the air around them. Kristina felt numb as she watched the figure flying off until it disappeared into the night.

She collapsed on the ground from exhaustion and again everything faded to black.

* * *

WHEN SHE WOKE UP, she was at home in her bed. She wasn't sure how much time had passed and much of the night had become a blur to her. In the days to come she would only be able to recall glimpses of that night. Most of the truth about what happened would be lost to her forever. She became stronger, more powerful in the craft, and the dark energy consumed her.

She remembered dancing in the woods with the elders around the fire as a rite of passage. She remembered someone holding up a snake or something, slicing it down the middle and having her drink its blood. As gross as it was, she understood the bloodletting part of voodoo. She couldn't remember much of anything else and no one talked about the wood ceremonies, so she didn't ask. It was gross enough knowing she probably drank the blood of a snake. She felt stronger, she couldn't wait to get out on the streets and test her new found abilities. Her mind was spinning in so many directions that when she stepped outside onto the street, she didn't notice all the fighting that had broken out around her. The same streets that were always filled with happy tourists laughing and having fun had now turned into people arguing on every corner and fighting in the middle of the road. Kristina stepped back onto her porch and looked around; it was as if the streets had taken on a new life of their own. A much darker evil feel than it had before. There was a crowd of people in an enormous fight. They were hitting one another repeatedly until their faces became a distorted blur of flesh and blood. The police rushed in to try and break it up but the crowd overwhelmed them. Some were arrested and others were carted away in ambulances. Bricks were being thrown into windows and everywhere she turned there was more violence. She had never seen anything like it before, not here, not in the peaceful streets of the French Quarter. Kristina's mother opened her front door and looked at her sternly, "Just go to school, it will pass our area by the time you are home. Now go, no one will harm you."

She hurried off through the streets stepping around everyone, trying not to make eye contact as the arguing continued on every corner with everyone that she passed by. She was amazed that no one approached her or said anything to her in the middle of this strange chaos. She finally reached the school and quickly went inside taking one final look back at the people in the streets. As she sat in her first class, she eagerly looked around for David but he wasn't at school this morning. "Maybe he had been caught up in the madness of the street fighting." She hoped not, he was the one person she looked forward to seeing at school every day. She didn't remember much about the night before but one thing hung on her every thought and that was that kiss! That once in a lifetime kiss from the boy of her dreams. Her thoughts faded everything around her away, except for David. She had been in love with him for as long as she could remember. After school she asked around but no one had seen him which struck her as odd since he never missed school. She hurried home and was happy to see that the streets seemed to have returned to their normalcy once again. Anxious to try out her own new strength in the craft, she quickly set up her things outside her house and waited for someone to stop by needing her services. "One day," she thought, "I'm going to have my own shop and people are going to come from all over just to see me." She was filled with a stronger power than she had ever felt before.

Just then a teenage girl came strolling down the street, laughing and holding hands with a young man. She stopped in front of Kristina and smiled, "Hey, do you read fortunes?"

"Why, yes I do," Kristina said eagerly. "Would you like yours read?"

The girl looked around for what she thought should be an old gypsy lady with a crystal ball. "Um, well, do you read them or like someone else, maybe older?"

Kristina raised her eyebrows and tilted her head looking downwards and smirked, "I can get my mom if you want. I'm actually much better. I know I'm probably your age but I've had the gift since I was six. I can even tell you something now if you want."

"Okay." the girl said, with a little bit of teenage curiosity. "I'm intrigued."

The girl sat down at the table with Kristina and the young man leaned over her, "I'll be back." He walked off and soon disappeared into one of the shops.

"Perfect!" Kristina said with a smile. "Take a seat. Now, give me your hand." She took the girls hand into hers and stared deeply into her eyes. "You're not from around here, right?"

"Well that's easy," the girl said, with a laugh.

Kristina glanced back up at her and smiled, "And that was… your boyfriend?"

"Easy again," the girl said, laughing harder. They were like two schoolgirls entertaining one another but a darkness filled Kristina.

"Okay, okay," Kristina said, and she closed her eyes and took a deep breath. The dark energy rushed through her veins and overtook her, and her eyes became black as night. "Oh, you're thinking of getting married? But your mother doesn't approve."

The girls face became expressionless as she stared at Kristina. She tried to pull her hand back but Kristina gripped onto her tightly.

"Oh, I see. You're…" and Kristina paused, her eyes became clear as she looked back at the girl.

She jerked her hand away, staring at Kristina and became very solemn, "I don't know what to do."

"Give me both your hands," Kristina said, and she closed her eyes. The power rushed through her stronger than before and a voice pushed its way inside of her head. She let go of the girl's hands and told her to wait outside. The girl sat in the chair nervously fidgeting as she awaited Kristina's return. When she came back and sat down, she had a black talisman and held it firmly in her hand.

"Keep this with you and it will keep you safe and protect you." She handed it to her. "Don't be scared, we all have a path and your baby deserves to find out his."

"His?" the girl said, a little surprised.

Kristina smiled, "I just know what I see. This baby isn't a mistake."

The girls sat there for a few minutes talking before the boyfriend returned, and it was time to leave.

"Hey," the girl looked back at Kristina with a smile. "If you're ever in St. Francisville, look me up. I'm Cindy or you can call me Mrs. Cole by then," and she laughed as she walked away.

Months went by, but no one ever heard from David again. His face became one of many on the posters that went up in the Quarter every year of missing teenagers, and it broke Kristina's heart. She tried every spell she knew to try and find him but everything was a dead end and she felt empty inside. Darkness consumed her and more than anything she wanted to leave the Quarter and never look back.

Over the next few years, she saved all of her money in hopes of starting her own shop far away from the city. Sometimes late at night she would still see the Hell Witch watching her or catch a glimpse of the shadow in her room. Sometimes, she would dream of David and it wasn't always good. Images of him haunted her every thought and living without him was unbearable to her. She wanted away from the Quarter more than ever.

Kristina and Cindy kept in touch on and off over the years. Cindy would come to the Quarter and Kristina would give her a reading. They would tell each other everything that was happening in their lives, and they became fast friends. The last time Kristina saw Cindy she had divorced her husband and was moving back to St. Francisville. Kristina made her a special talisman that had come to her in a dream. "Hang this on your car's rearview mirror. It will protect you and your son." That's what she thought it did, however, the darkness grew inside of her and the lines between good and evil became blurred.

The news of Cindy's death was shocking, and Kristina went to St. Francisville to pay her last respects. Once she saw the small town and met Charlotte, she decided to stay and they too became friends. Charlotte was fascinated with her and wanted to learn to read the tarot cards herself. Truth be known she wanted to learn everything she could from her. She missed her daughter terribly and somehow Kristina helped to fill that empty void.

She encouraged her to buy the bookstore and make it her own. "People around this town are a little stuck in the mud," she would say, "but they will come around. Just watch. Keep everything in the back and they will be coming to you!"

She was right. Slowly word got around and customers started to come in secretly, to see Kristina. She became so busy that she started to teach Charlotte everything she knew about voodoo, talismans and reading tarot cards. Before long, Charlotte was doing readings in the back of the store once a week. She found it exciting, and she and Kristina became very close. Kristina even gave Charlotte the purple talisman she had gotten from her grandmother years before, and told her to always keep it with her.

Kristina learned to control the darkness, and shoved it deep inside of her, but it pushed its way through from time to time. The darkness had a life of its own.

OPENING THE DOOR

*C*laire walked into the bookstore but Kristina was nowhere in sight. She walked throughout the shop, thumbing the books one by one as her eyes locked in on the door behind the counter. Glancing around for Kristina, she stepped behind the counter, closer to the door. She jiggled the knob but it was locked. Quickly she began to search under the counter for the key but was interrupted when Kristina stepped into the store. Jerking up, she quickly turned around, "I was just looking for you!" She moved out from behind the counter and smiled.

"Well, you found me," Kristina smirked.

Claire sat down at the small white table, "I wondered if I could talk to you, if you have the time?"

"Sure," Kristina replied, "Would you like a cup of coffee or tea?"

"No, thank you." Claire put her camera on the table and tried to figure out how to approach the subject. "This is going to sound strange but I need to talk to someone or I might actually go crazy." She fidgeted with the camera strap and searched

Kristina's face for reassurance, "I think there is something... evil in our house. I hear it late at night and I've seen things, things that I can't explain."

Kristina's expression became solemn as she sat back in her chair and stared at Claire.

"I know," Claire said, shaking her head and taking a deep breath. "It sounds ridiculous but I don't know what's happening and I feel like if I don't figure it out soon, someone could get hurt, if they haven't already."

"Claire," Kristina got up and locked the door of the shop. "Have I ever told you how I came to this town and how I met Charlotte?" She sat back down.

"No," Claire replied, siting up straight and hanging on her every word.

Kristina leaned across the table, staring intently at Claire. She took a deep breath, and grabbed her hand. "It was a long time ago. I met Cindy a few times in the Quarter, that's where I lived before. You see, where I grew up, some people were gifted and could do things with sorcery, using different elements. Most of them were known as street tellers or fortune tellers. My family comes from a long line that was gifted in the craft and practiced the religion of Vodun. My grandmother and great grandmother were taught as children in West Africa long before they made their way to New Orleans. You see Claire, I specialize in helping people with different things, such as talismans or charms that bring them good luck. I'm also quite gifted at reading tarot cards which can tell people their future. Visitors often came to our neighborhood just to see me or my mother."

"Like voodoo!" Claire said, as she jerked her hand back in surprise.

"Yes," Kristina laughed. "It's nothing to fear. That's how I met Cindy. We were young and she passed by me one day on the street and I read her fortune. We became friends and she visited me on and off for years until her accident. When I heard about it, I packed my things and came here and that's when I met Charlotte. She was always so kind to me." She took a deep breath and looked down for a moment, "Anyway, I was having my own problems and needed a bit of a change. I believe you and Jason had just left town or I would have met you back then. Charlotte was having a hard time with losing Cindy and I gave her a few things to help her relax. Before long, we became friends and she talked me into buying this bookstore. Truth is, we both needed someone at the time and our paths seemed almost destined to cross."

"So, wait, you do fortune telling and sell voodoo stuff out of this shop?" Claire asked, pointing at the table.

"Yes," Kristina answered. "But its kept pretty hush-hush. Some of the people in town are superstitious and others that come in here… well, they would just rather keep it private."

"So, what did Charlotte do here?" Claire asked curiously. She had decided not to mention anything about the symbols on the shed.

"Well, she was very interested in the craft and how it worked and even though she wasn't born with the gift, I was able to teach her a few things. After a while, she was able to read tarot cards pretty well and so once or twice a week, she would come in and do readings for people in the back room." Kristina got up and poured a cup of tea.

"That's what the back room is all about?" Claire asked. She looked over at the mysterious door behind the counter.

"Yes," Kristina said with a smile. "Among other things."

"So, this voodoo stuff. Is it for real or just a way to make extra money?" Claire snickered.

Kristina's expression changed immediately as she looked over at Claire, "Is there something in your house or is it your imagination?"

Claire stopped laughing, "Touché, I think there is something in my house."

"I've seen many things in my life," Kristina said, "Some good, some bad and some that can't be explained. I'll come to your house and take a look around myself. If there is something there, I will be able to sense it. I've dealt with an evil presence in my own life and you can keep it away if you know what you're dealing with. I'll stop by tomorrow in the afternoon. Will that work for you?"

"That would be great! Well, I've kept you long enough, I better get going." Claire said. She got up to leave but stopped just before opening the door. "Oh, this voodoo stuff. Does it have anything to do with symbols or anything like that?"

"No," Kristina replied, "It doesn't quite work like that. Why do you ask?"

"Oh nothing, just curious," Claire said, and she hugged Kristina goodbye before leaving the store. "I'll see you tomorrow and... thank you."

"No problem. Like I said, I consider you and Jason family."

As Claire left, she thought about everything Kristina had told her about Charlotte. She decided not to mention anything to her about the pictures either. At least now she knew what was really happening in the bookstore and how Charlotte was connected. It was almost lunch time when she received a call from Jason, "Claire, I'm sorry I can't find a substitute to cover for me. I'll catch a ride home as soon as I'm done with my last class."

Claire took a deep breath, "Do you want me to come back and pick you up?"

"No, that's alright," Jason said, "One of the other teachers passes right by our place. I was thinking of carpooling with him sometime anyway. I'll see you when I get home. I love you."

Just like that Claire was faced with being alone in the house again. "I think I'll pick up Sara early." She picked her up and they headed home for the rest of the afternoon.

"Can we go swimming?" Sara asked bouncing up and down in the back seat.

"Maybe," Claire replied, "buckle your seatbelt."

They returned home and as they got out of the car and started to walk inside the house, Claire felt an unusual gust of wind blow past them. She unlocked the door and as soon as they went inside, Sara ran up the stairs to put on her swimsuit. Earlier when Claire said maybe, all Sara heard in her mind was, "Definitely, as soon as we get home! Now run as fast as you can so we don't waste any time!"

"Wait," Claire said as she sat her things down on the table, "I said maybe. I have to do something first."

Sara put on her swimsuit anyway, grabbed her toys and stood by the backdoor to look out the window at the pool. "Now?" she asked eagerly.

"No, wait a few minutes and then we can go out," Claire replied, looking around the kitchen. She wanted to see if she could find tarot cards or anything like that in the attic. She grabbed her hammer and the bolt cutter and went upstairs. Carefully, one by one she pulled all three nails out of the attic door.

"Don't go outside!" she yelled down to Sara. She opened the door slowly, turned the light on and stepped inside the attic. She surveyed the boxes around the room and sat on floor as she began to rummage through them. She glanced over at the small locked door and picked up the bolt cutters. "It's worth a try." She pushed the boxes away from the small door and gripped the bolt cutters tightly on the lock. "Please God! I won't ask for anything else if you will please help me open this lock!" Suddenly the lock snapped in half and Claire fell backwards, eyes glued to the door. It was covered with dust and cobwebs and she brushed them away as she slowly turned the knob. Suddenly, a gust of wind blew from the hidden room as she pried the door open. She could barely see anything and reached over to grab a flashlight. She hit it on her hand a couple of times to get it to turn on, and shined it in the dark room. The light made its way to symbols that were carved into the wall and Claire froze. She leaned in just a bit to get a closer look when something in the corner caught her eye. She shined the light around the small room. There were bones of some sort in the corner, in the middle of a circle, with rocks all around it. She couldn't tell what she was looking at but it had been there long before Charlotte. The room held a stench and she started to cough. She backed out of the room and sat on the floor in the attic trying to catch her breath. When she lifted her head back up the door was shut with the lock firmly in place. She gasped and glared at the door, stunned. She grabbed at the bolt and glanced at the cutters on the floor. She scooted quickly away from the door and backed into a box knocking it over and spilling its contents out onto the floor. She looked down at the box and on it in black letters was written, CINDYS'. She jerked her head back up and stared at the locked door then began to try and stuff everything back in the box. A small wooden box had fallen out and she opened it. There was a purple rock of some sort, a black triangle looking thing and a photo of Cindy when she was younger, standing on the sidewalk in front of a townhouse with a beautiful black girl about the same age. They stood side by side smiling with their arms wrapped around each other and Cindy was holding something in her hand. There was something very familiar about the other girl. Just then she noticed the dark smudge behind Cindy in the photo. She stared at it intently for a few minutes. Suddenly the light in the attic went off and the door slammed shut.

"No!" screamed Claire. She got up and tried to find her way to the door but the attic was dark and the only light shining in was through a thin gray curtain covering the window. The boxes had been scattered about since she was digging through them earlier which left a trail for her to trip over as she frantically made her way to the attic door.

A whisper came out of the darkness, "Claire." Every muscle in her body tensed up and she froze. She could hear heavy breathing from inside the room and one by one footsteps slowly moved towards her.

She quickly reached up for the light and when she was able to flip the switch on, the breathing and footsteps stopped. She opened the door frantically and stepped back into the game room. She slammed it shut and grabbed the nails and began nailing it back as quickly as she could.

"Sara!" she called out, but Sara was nowhere to be seen. She ran downstairs and through the house but couldn't find her anywhere.

"Sara!" she yelled out again. When she ran through the living room, she noticed the back door was open, and looked outside to see Sara sitting on the edge of the pool with her feet in the water.

"Sara!" she screamed.

Sara turned around quickly and ran towards the house. "I didn't get in. I was waiting," she said nervously.

"You know not to go outside! I told you not to open the door!" Claire yelled, as she reached for Sara, and pulled her into the house, slamming the back door shut.

"I just wanted to put my feet in the water," Sara said, trying to explain her innocence.

"Now, no swimming at all!" Claire said. "You have to listen. Now change your clothes!"

Sara stomped up the stairs to her room, crying as she threw her toys down and slammed her bedroom door. "You never let me do anything!" she yelled from behind the door.

Claire sat down on the couch in somewhat of a daze as she put her head in the palm of her hands, took a deep breath and wiped her face. "Shit! Sara, wait!" she yelled, as she ran up the stairs. "Come down!" She didn't hear anything from Sara's room as she grabbed the door and pushed it open. Sara was sitting on her bed playing with the dragonfly, still pouting over the pool. "Sara, why don't you come downstairs with me? You can watch cartoons in the living room. Maybe we can swim tomorrow." She grabbed Sara's hand and lead her back downstairs, glancing back at the attic door. It remained nailed shut.

She put cartoons on in the living room for Sara and went into the kitchen to cook dinner. The house was quiet except for occasional laughter from Sara, and Claire's mind shoveled through everything she had seen in the attic and of the photo. "Kristina, it had to be. Kristina and Cindy. But the smudge, the shadow, the door! The door was locked but I know what I saw. Just keep it together."

Later, Sara made her way into the kitchen. She was a welcoming distraction for Claire who was finishing up a pot of stew.

"Hungry?" Claire asked Sara with a smile.

"Yes," Sara said, still pouting from earlier. "Can we go swimming now?"

"No," Claire said. She shot her a look that said this is the last time I want to hear about the pool. "You have to listen Sara. I told you not to go outside. You could have fallen in. What if you drowned? I wouldn't have even known you were out there."

"Okay," Sara said, sulking back in her chair, "I'm sorry, but I'm a really good swimmer, especially with my floaties on."

"I know," Claire said, reaching down and giving her a quick hug, "but you have to listen to me and when you don't there are consequences for you misbehaving."

Jason opened the door and Claire ran up and hugged him tightly as she let out a sigh of relief. "Jason, you're home."

He kissed her cheek, "You okay?"

"Yes, it's just today, I went in the attic and..."

"You went in the attic?" He pushed her back a bit and looked at her surprisingly. "I thought you nailed it shut?"

"I un-nailed it," Claire replied. "I thought maybe I could find something to help make sense of... anything. The door..."

"Well, what did you find?" Jason interrupted as he sat down at the table.

"Daddy!" Sara yelled, and she flung her arms around Jason's neck and hopped on his lap.

Claire looked at Sara and decided not to discuss it in front of her. She didn't want to scare Sara, and so far they had managed to keep everything from her. "Nothing, a bunch of boxes. I nailed it back," Claire said, looking down and setting the plates of food on the table. "I might look again tomorrow but for now, I think I'll leave it alone."

Jason put Sara in the chair next to him and they began to eat. He glanced back at Claire, "Are you sure you're okay? You look pale."

"I'm okay. Just a long day, this house..." She shook her head.

"Hey, it's okay. Everything is going to be okay," he said.

"I know." She didn't tell Jason about what had happened in the attic or about what she had learned from Kristina. She was worried enough about whatever she had seen behind the small locked door inside the attic.

That night Claire tucked Sara into bed, closed her door and checked the attic door. Still nailed shut. She went downstairs to their bedroom.

"Where is Sara?" Jason asked sitting up in bed and looking anxiously at Claire.

"We have to let her sleep in her own room," she replied. She grabbed her clothes and began to dress for bed, "I don't want her to know anything that is going on in this house. It will just scare her and it doesn't seem to mess with her anyway. Honestly she seems safer in her room than we are in ours."

"That's ridiculous, she should be in here with us." Jason said reluctantly.

"I don't want her to hear us," Claire whispered.

"Hm. Okay, crawl in." He smiled and pulled back the covers.

"Yeah. No, get up." Claire grabbed her robe.

"What?" Jason sat up.

"Get up. I need to show you something. Come on." She grabbed Jason's hand and led him up the stairs. Stopping quickly to check on Sara, she opened her door, but she was fast asleep, doll in one hand and the little dragonfly in the other. She closed the door quietly.

"Claire, what are we doing up here?" Jason walked towards the pool table.

Claire moved quickly towards the attic and grabbed the hammer and began un-nailing the door. "Jason, earlier... I lied. I mean I did find something in the attic. The door, the small door... I took the bolt off and there was something in that room but I fell and something whispered and there were some sort of bones. And then, Jason... it was shut, like I never opened it." She stopped to look up at him but his mouth was open and his eyes squinted in disbelief.

"You didn't think you might want to tell me that when I first got home?" He wiped his forehead in frustration.

She took the last nail out and opened the door.

"Why are we going in here?" Jason said as she pushed him towards the door. "Alright." He stepped in the attic and turned the light on. There was nothing but a room full of boxes and an old attic smell.

Claire picked up the bolt cutters and moved towards the small door. Jason took them from her. "Here, let me see it." He gripped the lock tightly and squeezed until the lock broke off and fell on the floor. Claire handed him the flashlight and he shinned it in the small room. It was full of insulation so thick that you could see nothing else. Claire jerked the light back, frantically searching the room with her eyes, "Jason, it's gone! It's all gone! It was here! Bones in a circle and the symbols... I don't understand." She stepped back away from the door as Jason closed it shut.

"Claire, are you sure you were awake? I mean this house, the dreams..." He put his hand on her arm but she jerked it away.

"Jason, I was awake." She turned around and walked out of the attic with Jason close behind her. She shut the door and picked up a nail.

"Really? Claire, I believe you but the nails don't do anything." He tried to pick up the hammer but she jerked it from him.

"It keeps the door shut," she said, and she nailed all three nails in before checking on Sara one last time.

They went downstairs and crawled back into bed. "Claire, I believe you but remember what Gabriel said? Don't pay it any attention. The more attention you give it, the more it will mess with you? Listen, you're up there digging in the attic, nailing and un-nailing. Don't you think that might be showing it some attention? Stay out of the attic." Jason rolled over and turned off their light.

* * *

A DARK FIGURE moved through the house and into Jason and Claire's room. It crept next to Claire's side of the bed and ran its fingers across her face. Claire rolled over in her sleep, moving up closer to Jason.

The shadow moved slowly around the bed and stopped to hover over Jason's body. It tilted its head upwards and its mouth elongated as whispers flooded the air. He began to dream.

HE WAS FLOATING *in the blue water of the swimming pool, looking up at the stars. A gentle wind blew across his face. Unexpectedly,*

something grabbed a hold of his leg and jerked him down into the
water. He gasped a quick breath before being dragged down
towards the bottom of the pool. He looked beneath him but there
was no bottom in sight, just a black empty void. He tried not to
panic as he fought to pull himself free from the hand that was
wrapped around his leg. He could see the light from the top of the
water fading farther and farther away. He frantically tried to
break free, reaching down and trying to pry the thing off of him.
His eyes searched the water around him. He saw a black figure
swimming towards him through the water with piercing red eyes.
He tried to move but the hand on his leg held him firmly in place.
As it swam past him, it reached out and clawed his chest with its
long sharp nails and blood flowed from Jason's body out into the
water. He looked over to see another dark figure swimming
towards him from the opposite direction with hollow blue eyes and
flowing hair. It swam quickly by him reaching out with its nails
and swiping them across his chest. Jason could feel the stinging
burn of each hit. He struggled to hold his breath. He looked above
through the water, towards the light shining in from above and his
body began to tremble. There were five different shadow figures
swimming above, each with their own terrifying shapes, with
large gnashing teeth, sharp claws and different color eyes, circling
all around him and one by one they started to viciously swim by
him cutting him to pieces. Jason was horrified, the flesh was being
ripped from his bones and his blood poured out into the water
turning it a dark murky red. He tried to scream out, but when he
did the bloody water filled his mouth and as he gasped for air,
everything faded to black. Suddenly he awoke.

"No!" screamed Jason, and he jumped up covered with sweat
from the dream.

"Jason," Claire said, as she awoke. "Are you okay?"

"Shit!" Jason said, jumping out of bed, "Shit, shit, shit!" He got up and went into the bathroom and pulled up his shirt, but the only marks were the ones that were still there from a few nights before.

Claire walked into the bathroom and put her hand on Jason's shoulder, "Jason, are you okay?" "Just a dream, just a dream." Jason said, shaking his head and turning around to hug Claire. Suddenly, they heard footsteps above them in the house.

"Shhh," Jason said, walking back into the bedroom. "Listen." They heard the footsteps again as if someone was walking across the attic floor above them.

"Go see what it is," Claire said sitting down on the bed looking at Jason.

Jason cocked his head sideways and looked back at her, "You nailed the door shut, right?" he whispered.

"Yes." Claire said, staring up at the ceiling.

"Then it's not going anywhere." Jason said, laying back on the bed and staring upward. They lay there listening until the sound of the footsteps stopped and then they looked at each other and Jason turned the television on.

"Turn on the Christian channel," Claire said jokingly, but also a little serious. "Pastor Gabriel said it would help keep things away at night."

"Christian channel it is!" Jason said, and he quickly flipped it to a preacher giving a nightly gospel lesson.

Claire sat up in bed and looked at Jason with a worried look on her face, "Jason, you should go check on Sara."

"You're right," he got up and slowly walked up the stairs and opened Sara's door and looked in. "This is the worst part about being the man," he thought, "We're always the first to die." Sara was sleeping sound holding her doll and the little dragonfly. Jason closed the door shut, went back downstairs and crawled back into bed with Claire.

"She's fine," he said moving up next to Claire and holding her in his arms. "At least someone can sleep in this house."

"Thank you" Claire said, laying her head on Jason's chest.

Jason looked down at Claire, "For what?"

"For not making me go," Claire smiled.

Jason laughed but they were both still on edge. They stared up at the ceiling but the house was quiet and eventually they fell asleep.

FLASHBACK

The next morning Jason dropped Sara off at the daycare, while Claire worked in the darkroom to finish up the pictures she had taken of the town. She knew Kristina would be coming by today and the morning seem to drag on forever. Finally, just after lunch Kristina showed up knocking on the front door.

"Come in," Claire said, feeling a little bit of relief that she had finally arrived.

"Hello," Kristina replied, walking into the room and laying her jacket on the chair.

Claire walked closely behind Kristina. "Would you like something to drink or…"

"No, thank you," Kristina interrupted, "I'm sorry, it's just, this is the first time I've been here since I found Charlotte. The house was quiet much like it is today."

She walked around the house looking at all the things of Charlotte's still left on the shelves.

"Well, do you sense anything?" Claire asked.

"It doesn't work like that," Kristina grinned, looking back at Claire.

She walked around and finally moved towards the stairs but said nothing as Claire walked closely behind her.

"The attic," Claire started, looking up the stairs. "I feel like whatever it is, lives in there and…"

"Yes, let's take a better look," Kristina said, before Claire could finish her sentence.

As they walked up the stairs Claire remembered the nails in the attic door.

"Oh, wait here!" she exclaimed as she ran back down the stairs.

Kristina stood at the top of the stairs looking across at the attic door, but as she started towards the attic she stopped and turned back and looked towards Sara's room. She opened the bedroom door and looked inside. All of Sara's toys were scattered on the floor throughout the room. She walked inside the bedroom and an old familiar feeling, that she hadn't felt in a long time, came over her.

"I got it!" Claire said, standing in front of Sara's doorway.

"What?" Kristina asked, turning back and looking at Claire.

"The attic, I got it," Claire said. "Come on, I'll show you."

Kristina walked out of the bedroom and gave it one final glance and then followed Claire to the attic.

"I nailed it shut, because it kept opening and, well…" Claire anxiously removed the nails from the door.

"You nailed it shut?" Kristina asked, raising her eyebrows and looking at Claire.

"Yes," answered Claire, feeling a little foolish as she opened the door. "It seemed to stay shut."

"Of course, it would," Kristina said, as she stepped into the room.

The attic was quiet and dim and Claire turned on the light stepping in behind Kristina.

The boxes were still scattered around from before and Kristina and Claire stepped over them making their way around the attic. Kristina walked over to the window and looked out at the backyard. It was a sunny day and the trees were blowing in the wind. You could see the pool and the pond from the window and Kristina stood starting out of it for a few minutes while her mind began to wander.

"Anything?" Claire asked, reaching down to pick up the wooden box. "Over here, this door was open yesterday and I thought I saw something but last night when Jason opened it there was nothing there." She pointed down to the little door inside the attic that was shut.

Kristina stood still looking out of the window of the attic staring towards the pond almost mesmerized.

"Kristina?" Claire asked. "Are you okay? Um, I found this box with this picture of Cindy." She picked up the box off the floor and took out the picture. "Here it is! Is this by any chance you?" She pointed to the girl standing on the sidewalk in the picture with Cindy.

Kristina took the picture and looked at it for minute. "Yes as a matter of fact it is. It has been a long time since this picture was taken," she laughed. "We were so young." She smiled and looked down and noticed the purple talisman in the box on the floor next to the black triangle piece. She reached down and picked it up, "The talisman, that explains it." She took a deep breath and put it back in the box.

"Explains what?" Claire asked, looking at Kristina and then back at the rock. "Do you know what that is?"

Kristina turned back around to the window and stared again out into the backyard. "Yes, I gave it to Charlotte a while back. She must have just packed it away."

Claire looked at Kristina searching the expression on her face, "Kristina? You said 'that explains it'. That explains what?"

Kristina didn't answer. The pond seemed hypnotic and she couldn't take her eyes from its direction as her mind began to drift farther away. All of the sudden Kristina gasped and held her hand tightly on the window seal. She could see flashes going through her mind of a night long ago. One she had deeply tried to forget. A flash of the night and the fog and the beast standing before her as a young girl. A flash of her kneeling down before the beast and drinking from the cup, as the red substance ran down her chin. She could almost taste it in her mouth and her stomach began to feel weak. Then a flash she had not remembered before of David lying on the ground in the circle with stones surrounding him. His body was ripped apart and he was covered in blood. A thousand voices filled her mind, "GET OUT!" Kristina gasped as she realized for the first time the truth behind that night and, horrified, she turned back towards Claire.

"I can't be here," Kristina said, clearly shaken. "I can't help you. I'm sorry."

She walked quickly from the attic, dropping the picture on the floor. As she passed Sara's door, it slammed shut by itself. She looked back towards Claire who had jumped back against the pool table when the door closed. She quickly turned and went down the stairs with Claire following close behind.

"Wait," Claire said. "Are you okay? Did you see the door? What did you see? Please stop, wait a minute. Kristina!"

But Kristina continued to the front door grabbing her coat and as she reached the front porch she stopped and looked at Claire. Claire stood looking at her confused and desperate in the doorway.

"Claire, I'm sorry," Kristina said, as she wiped a tear away from her face. "For more than you know. I can't help you, please, I'm sorry. I just can't be here," and with that Kristina quickly walked to her car, got in, and drove away with Claire standing on the front porch helplessly watching her leave.

Claire stared down the road as Kristina's car disappeared from her sight. She turned around and stepped back into the house and closed the door. "What now?" she thought.

As Kristina reached the bookstore, she unlocked the door and went into the back room. "Why?" she cried out as she fell upon the floor. "There is always a price," whispered a deep voice, and the door slowly closed shut to the room with Kristina inside.

* * *

CLAIRE WALKED BACK up the stairs to shut the attic. She stopped at Sara's door and opened it but nothing was there but a heap of Sara's toys thrown about. She Stepped into the attic and looked over at the small door. She reached down, took a deep breath and opened it again. She grabbed the flashlight and shined it into the room. This time there was no insulation and the symbols were again carved into the wall. She turned her head quickly to the corner of the small room and lying on the floor was a child about Sara's age. She appeared asleep but the stones were circled around her. "Hey!" Claire shouted, and she reached for the girl but when she touched her the girl's head turned, and her eyes were black. Her mouth dropped open, and a loud groan filled the room. Claire screamed and jumped out of the room back into the attic and slammed the little door shut. She jumped up and quickly left the attic. She didn't even stop to turn the light off, she slammed the door and nailed it back. As silly as it seemed to her, it still gave her some sense of control. She opened a drawer and put the hammer inside but noticed an old notebook she hadn't seen before. She grabbed it and walked back down the stairs and sat on the couch in the living room and began to look through it. It was full of budgets and recipes and notes about jobs. It had a picture of Jason and Cindy and an old birthday card addressed to Cindy from Charlotte. "This must have been Cindy's," she thought, and she continued to look through the pages until she came to a short passage.

. . .

'JUNE 5TH

The demon has followed me for days. I have done everything I can and still it haunts my every move. I have no one to turn to and I feel like I am at a complete loss. I have only spoken to my mother about the visions. While Jason is in college, I feel he is safe for now. I don't want to drag him into this; however, he should be warned. My mom seems to be experiencing things of her own. I don't want to sleep and I can no longer force myself to stay awake. The demon attacks me both day and night. I hear the hounds calling more now as if they are getting closer and it terrifies me. I see the shadows everywhere and I know why they have come. I have seen it in a dream, they are searching for her'

THE PARAGRAPH SEEMED to stop mid-sentence, as if Cindy was interrupted writing and never had the chance to finish. "June 5th?" Claire thought. "Two days before Cindy's car accident on the bridge." Claire thought it best to put the notebook away. She wasn't sure if she should tell Jason or not. He had been through a lot getting past his mother's death and this would only raise more questions. As she walked around, picking up the scattered toys Sara had left lying about, she kept thinking about the passage that Cindy had written. "What did she know and what did she see in her dream," she thought. "Searching for who? Why did Kristina act so strange and what was that in the attic?"

* * *

LATER THAT EVENING, Jason returned home with Sara and they all talked about their day, but Claire was careful to leave out Kristina's visit and the notebook. Soon it was time for bed and Jason read Sara a story and tucked her in for the night.

"Goodnight Sara," Jason said kissing her on the head.

"Night Daddy," Sara replied as she snuggled her doll close

and closed her eyes. As she turned over in her bed the little dragonfly fell to the floor.

That night while they slept a dark shadow moved through the house. Sara's door slowly opened and a dark figure came into her room and stood next to her bed staring down at her. It put its hand on Sara's chest, tilting its head upwards, its mouth elongated and whispers filled the air. Sara started to toss in her sleep as she began to dream.

She was standing alone at the top of the stairs. She could barely see around the room, with only the dim light shining through the window from the moon. The house was quiet and empty and suddenly she heard a voice call out to her. "Sara." It sounded like Claire. "Mom!" Sara shouted, "Where are you?"

As Sara began to walk through the house searching for Claire, the rooms seemed to change around every corner. She ran down the stairs and found herself standing in the kitchen and when she came out of the kitchen and into the next room, she found herself suddenly back upstairs, standing at the end of the hallway, as if she had just stepped out of one of the bedrooms. Fear overtook her as she ran down the stairs again calling out, "Mom!" She continued to search the house but as soon as she reached the bottom of the stairs, she found herself standing inside the attic with the door locked. She looked around the room and tried to turn the doorknob but it wouldn't open. "Mom!" she yelled, but no one came. The attic was quiet and she could see the boxes scattered around on the floor. Her heart began to beat faster as her eyes searched quickly around the small room. She carefully stepped over the boxes and walked towards the window and looked out into the backyard. She could see a young girl that looked about her size and age with long blonde hair, standing outside by the pond. The girl began to walk towards the field and the trees, her hair blowing from the night wind. She was

*wearing the same pink nightgown with butterflies that Sara
had on.*

*She couldn't take her eyes off of the little girl and every muscle
in her body began to tense up. Every breath she took became
shorter and faster and she could feel her heart pulsing inside of
her chest. The little girl stopped, turned and looked back up
towards the house, directly at Sara. She had a wicked grin on her
face and Sara realized the girl looked exactly like her. Frightened,
she jumped back and let out a loud scream, "Mom! Dad! Help me!"
She couldn't look away as the little girl turned back and walked
farther into the field until Sara couldn't see her anymore. Tears
ran down Sara's face as she quickly moved away from the window
and again, let out a loud scream. She ran towards the attic door,
stumbling over boxes in the dark. She grabbed the doorknob and
struggled to turn it and open the door but it was still locked and
would not budge. She began pounding on the door until she heard
the screeching of a door opening across the room and a chill ran
through her body as she slowly turned around. The small door
inside the attic opened and a thousand whispers filled the room,
"Sara. The white-eyed demon is coming."*

SHE WOKE up and sat straight up in bed, screaming as loud as
she could, "Mom!" As she looked towards her bedroom door it
slowly closed shut. Sara pulled the blanket over her head and sat
still in the bed, too afraid to move. She could hear heavy
breathing inside the room and footsteps that sounded like they
were moving closer to her bed. All of the sudden her door burst
open and Claire stepped inside, turning on the light.

"Are you okay?" she asked frantically moving towards Sara.

"I had a bad dream," cried Sara still frightened. She was
shaking and holding on to her doll. "The woods."

"It's okay," Claire said, trying to comfort her. "It was just a dream. Why don't you come downstairs and sleep with me and Daddy?"

"Dragonfly!" screamed Sara. "Where is it?!"

Claire reached down and grabbed the little dragonfly off the floor and handed it to her, "It's okay, here. Everything is okay." She reached down and grabbed Sara out of bed and carried her downstairs. Sara clung to her tightly.

They walked back down the stairs and Claire put Sara in bed next to Jason. She crawled in next to her and held her close as they both drifted off to sleep.

DEVIL'S DOG

*I*t was raining when Jason awoke the next morning. He was running late, so he quickly jumped into the shower to get ready for work. Claire went into the kitchen to cook breakfast as Sara lay on the bed still asleep.

"No time to eat," Jason said, as he grabbed a quick cup of coffee and headed towards the front door. "I'll call you later."

"Bye," Claire said, looking at all the food she had just prepared.

She began walking around the house picking up toys and thinking about everything she was going to do that day. "The bookstore is a definite stop," she thought. And she went to wake Sara up before her breakfast became too cold to eat. She wondered again if she had done the right thing keeping the notebook from Jason.

* * *

JASON WAS DRIVING to work when he passed the bridge on Old River Road, he turned his head for just a moment to look at the bridge and when he turned back something was in the middle of the road. He slammed on his brakes and as his car slid to a stop in the rain, he saw the big black Rottweiler dog, sitting in the middle of the road. His car stopped just feet away from the dog, however the dog didn't move but instead, it sat there, locking eyes with Jason. Suddenly, he hit the gas pedal and went full speed ahead but as he drove towards the dog it vanished from sight. Jason hit the brakes again and looked all around the car but through the rain beating down heavily, he could see nothing. He took a deep breath and nervously continued on his way to work.

He reached the school, got out of his car and grabbed his umbrella and briefcase and as he ran across the parking lot, he could hear several dogs barking in the distance. He looked around as he kept running towards the front door of the school, the barking seemed to get closer to him. Just as he stepped inside the doors, he turned and looked across the parking lot and through the scattered rain storm he could see nothing. Jason tried to catch his breath as he wiped the rain off his face with his hands and took one last look at the parking lot before he went into class.

* * *

AFTER CLAIRE and Sara had dressed for the day, they headed into town. Claire dropped Sara off at daycare and headed to the bookstore to speak with Kristina. She was anxious to find out what had happened the day before in the attic. As she reached the bookstore, she was surprised to see a sign hanging in the window that read 'Closed'. She stepped back and looked at her watch, "11:15," she thought. "The bookstore should be open." She knocked on the door but no one came, and after a few minutes, she decided to return home and try and get some work done.

* * *

CLAIRE WAS in the darkroom looking through pictures when she heard a loud banging noise coming from the next room. It sounded like someone stomping down the lower half of the stairs. Startled, she jumped back against her table and quickly reached for the darkroom door and locked it. She stared at the door and took a couple of steps back, listening for any other sound coming from the house, but she heard nothing. She reached for her cell phone, staring at the door and called Jason.

"Jason! I think someone is in the house." Claire whispered. Her voice was shaking and every muscle in her body tensed up.

"What's happening?" Jason asked, as he got up and stepped out of the classroom. He stood in the hall nervously awaiting her response.

Claire sat quietly in the darkroom listening for any noises in the house. "I'm in the darkroom and I heard something, it sounded like someone stomping down the stairs, but the house is locked. What if it's whoever put those symbols on the shed? Jason, I'm scared."

"Hold on! Don't leave the darkroom and stay on the phone with me. I'll call the sheriff on the other phone," Jason replied as he quickly walked down the hall to the teachers' lounge and picked up the phone.

Claire could hear Jason calling the sheriff's office, but they couldn't get there quick enough for her. All kinds of thoughts were running through her mind. If someone was in the house and reached her first, what would happen? She was sure someone had broken in and, being so far back in the bayou, it would take the sheriff a while to reach her. She started to search around the darkroom for anything she could use as a weapon in case someone came through the darkroom door, but there was nothing. Just a table and sinks and a clothesline hanging across the room with pictures clipped on it to dry. Not even a bat or a club, nothing she could use to hit anyone should they come in. She felt helpless and afraid and it terrified her that she had no way to defend herself. Jason stayed on the phone with her trying to comfort her as she waited what seemed like forever for the sheriff to arrive.

"Claire! The sheriff is outside, run for the front door!" Jason said.

Claire darted out of the room and ran quickly to the front door to let the sheriff and his deputy in. After they entered the house and looked around, they found nothing. Claire walked closely behind them and told them what she had heard and as they opened every room one by one. They found no one. All the doors in the house were locked and the windows were closed with no sign of anyone breaking in.

"Looks all clear, ma'am," the deputy said, as he filled out the rest of his report.

"I know what I heard," Claire said, wiping the tears from her eyes and still visibly shaking.

"You don't have a ghost, do you?" the sheriff joked. He smiled as they walked toward the front door to leave.

That was the first time that it dawned on Claire that it could have been that thing that was in their house. It sounded so much like a person on the stairs, that she never gave it a thought that it could have been something entirely different.

"No," she answered to the sheriff, shaking her head. "No ghost."

As the sheriff and his deputy drove away, she called Jason to let him know everything was okay and stepped back into the house and took another looked around. "That thing," she thought. "Well, I'm not staying in here." She grabbed her purse and her keys and headed out the door to drive into town. All she could think of was how much she wanted to get out of the house for a while. If it was, whatever was terrorizing her home, then she wasn't staying there alone. As she drove into town, she thought she would try Kristina again.

As she reached the bookstore, she was relieved to find it open, and Kristina standing inside at the counter. If nothing else she could have a cup of tea and get away from the house for a couple of hours. She decided not to bring up anything about Kristina's visit to her house before and see if she would open up to her on her own.

"Hello," Kristina said, smiling at Claire. "What brings you in today?" As if she didn't know.

"Just wanted out of the house," Claire said, taking a seat at her usual table in the back of the bookstore. "You doing okay?"

"Yes," Kristina replied, as she poured Claire a cup of tea and sat it down on the table. "I'm sorry about the house, yesterday... I really don't think I'm the person that can help you. Charlotte had once told me she was hearing things in the house and I told her what I would do, but honestly it could have made things worse. I would rather not give you bad direction. If anything," she paused for a few seconds, "I would call on Pastor Gabriel, if anyone can help you, honestly, maybe he can."

Reluctantly, Claire dropped the subject. She could see Kristina didn't want to talk too much about it which made her think again. What did she see in the attic that would frighten her? She drank the rest of her tea, making more small talk to pass the time as her thoughts drifted to the closed door behind the counter. "What is in that room?" she thought.

"Claire, would you mind keeping an eye on the store while I run across the street and pick up lunch?" Kristina asked, getting up from the table and grabbing her purse from behind the counter.

Claire took another sip of her tea, "Sure, no problem."

As Kristina left the store Claire looked at the closed door to the room and walked slowly behind the counter and turned the knob but the door was locked. She began to look around the counter and as she ran her hand under the shelf, she discovered a key. She looked out the window and could see Kristina was still waiting across the street in the café. She quickly grabbed the key and put it in the keyhole and turned it. With a click, the door unlocked. Surprised, Claire slowly opened the door to the back room. It was dark and she could see nothing as she stepped inside and felt along the wall for a light switch. Finally, she felt the switch, and turned the light on. As she looked around the room, a strange feeling came over her. The room was lined with wooden shelves full of different objects. Claire walked through the room running her fingers along the shelves touching all the trinkets that filled the dim lit room. There were books and dolls sitting on one shelf and stones and small black bags full of something she couldn't quite make out, sitting on another. There were incense and bottles full of different liquids, and a book on the bottom shelf that she picked up and opened.

'Oct. 5. The dreams are getting worse and even the priest is at a loss. He left for the Vatican today in search of answers and I fear the Hell Witch's words, the warning of the fifth demon with red eyes coming. I don't know what it means and I pray the priest returns before it is too late.'

Claire closed the book and set it back on the shelf. She wasn't sure how long Kristina would be gone and as she came to the back of the room, her eyes locked on a glass case that had a statue figure sitting inside of it. Along the sides of the case were markings and symbols written along the trim and flowers and incense burned at the bottom along the floor in front of it. Claire's eyes widened as she looked at the statue of a man's body with a bull's head sitting Indian style, inside the case. It had big black horns and big dark black eyes that seem to stare right through her. It had hooves instead of feet and distorted hands with long black claws. Inside the glass at the top of the case were two red lights that shined down on the statue and black flowers, long sticks and some sort of grass that filled the bottom. There was an empty brown bowl made of clay, sitting at the feet of the beast. Claire gasped and backed away from the glass case and as she turned around Kristina was standing inside the room.

"What are you doing in here?!" Kristina asked, squinting her eyes at Claire with a look of agitation on her face.

"I, I, I'm sorry," Claire said, taking a deep breath and walking quickly towards the door of the room.

"I mean, I thought I heard something so I..." Claire glanced back in an attempt to explain the situation.

"Unlocked the door?!" Kristina interrupted. "You have no right to be in here!" Kristina followed closely behind Claire as the anger started to build up from Claire's once again invasive curiosity.

"I'm sorry," Claire said, nervously looking back at Kristina who was fully annoyed at this point, "I should go." Claire walked as quickly as she could to the front of the bookstore without saying another word as Kristina watched her leave in silence. She closed the door to the back room and stood at the counter saying nothing.

Claire quickly walked to her car and got in, still thinking of what she had seen in the back room. She was unable to get the image of the beast out of her thoughts and it didn't escape her the resemblance of the symbols.

"What was that thing? Why was it there?" the thoughts raced through her mind. She decided to stop at the church and see if Pastor Gabriel was back from his trip before returning home.

As she pulled her car into the parking lot of the church, she could see the pastor sitting outside on the steps reading from a book and enjoying the fresh air. He looked more concerned than usual and had a strange look of worry on his face that Claire was not use to seeing. She tried to put her feelings aside but the fear and shock ran through her like an adrenalin rush from what she had seen in the back of the bookstore.

"Pastor Gabriel," Claire called, as she began walking towards him.

"Claire," Gabriel replied, closing the book and setting it down on the steps, "It's great to see you. I was going to call you and Jason today. I just got back in town yesterday." He noticed Claire was upset, "Are you okay?"

"I'm okay," Claire said. "Still here," she said jokingly, trying to hide the uncertainty from her face. "Actually, I wondered if you had found anything out on your trip? And I…" she stopped. She wondered if she should mention the bookstore and the statue or anything else that had happened since they had last spoke. She didn't actually know what she had seen in the bookstore or her attic and wasn't sure she wanted to add fuel to fire with Kristina by disclosing her speculations. "I just need your help," she said finally, taking a deep breath.

Gabriel looked at her and could tell there was much more to her story than was being told.

"Claire, like I said before, I was actually going to call you and Jason today. I spoke to my friend in the Quarters, Father Taylor, he is over at St. Anne's catholic church. He wanted to come down and speak to you and Jason directly. I believe he can help. He has worked closely with situations that are similar to yours and he knows how to deal with this much better than I do. Is it okay if we come out to the house tomorrow night when he arrives?" He looked at her with concern.

Claire searched Gabriel's face for clues. "Of course, but I mean, is everything okay? Please if you found something out… I'm losing my mind out there."

"It's okay Claire, we will be by tomorrow night around six. I just want to finish some things up around here first and Father

Taylor wants to take a look for himself to make sure it's what he thinks it is. I promise you this, you will have answers." Gabriel tried to give her a comforting smile but the look of seriousness on his face had already burned an impression into Claire's mind. He took Claire's hand and held it firmly, "Keep your faith strong. Everything will be alright and remember, God is stronger than anything we might be dealing with."

Those words hung in the air as Claire shook his hand and sat down on the steps next to Gabriel and let out a deep breath. She had more questions now than when she first got there but the thought that the priest was coming sounded promising to her.

She looked at Gabriel and shook her head, "I thought coming back would be easier. The feel of being home again. The green grass of the fields and the smell of the flowers blowing through the breeze in the meadows. The sun glistening down on the water in the bayou and the sound of the crickets at night. I thought it would bring Jason and I some peace after losing Charlotte, to be in the house." She looked down as tears began to fall from her eyes and roll down her face. "It's been anything but peaceful. It's like this ongoing nightmare that I can't wake up from. Things move in the house at night and during the day. Sounds, stomps, doors opening and closing, breathing. Sometimes I'll be in the kitchen cooking and my hair will move and I can feel something's hot breath on my neck. I fear being asleep. I don't know if it's in the room with me or what it will do to me or worse to Sara or Jason. I wish we would have never come back."

Gabriel wrapped his arm around Claire's shoulder, "Claire, Father Taylor can help. He knows what you're dealing with firsthand. Everything is going to be okay. I know it's been hard out there but please just hold on and it will get better. I promise."

Claire looked at Gabriel, "I feel like it's connected to the bookstore. I can't explain it but Charlotte had a connection to the store and..."

Gabriel interrupted her, "The bookstore, it opens a lot of doors. People turn to different things to find comfort. What looks like a quick fix to their problems can sometimes bring them more troubles than they had to start with. I wish people would choose the door to the church instead. It's the only real place that holds all the answers to their pain. Still, they turn to other things: booze, drugs, the bookstore... all doors that open to let bad things in." the pastor shook his head. "Have faith, be strong and together we'll get rid of whatever is in your house."

"Thank you," Claire said, as she wiped her eyes and got up to leave.

"Claire, there is still peace around you," Gabriel tried to say with a comforting look. "This will all soon be over and you will have those days in the bayou that you and Jason deserve."

Claire got up and walked to her car glancing back to give the pastor a smile before leaving.

ALTAR

*C*laire returned home with Sara. As they went into the house, she smelled something rotten. Claire stepped into the living room, and the stench was overwhelming. She coughed and covered her nose.

"Mommy, something stinks!" Sara said.

"Go outside," Claire said, as she opened the back door.

Sara ran out the door and stood in the grass looking back at the house to see if Claire would follow her. She looked around the yard and back towards the pond and field which made her think of the dream.

"Mom!" Sara yelled. "Are you coming?!"

She looked back towards the pond again, and thought she saw something move just beyond the shack.

Claire walked around the inside of the house, looking for the source of the smell. When she reached the kitchen, she noticed the gas burners were turned on but the flame was out. She quickly reached for the knobs and turned them off. "No wonder." She thought. She went around and opened all the windows and doors to let the gas fumes out of the house, and then stepped into the backyard.

"Sara!" she called out, but Sara was nowhere in sight. Claire looked around the yard and then stepped back into the house.

"Sara, are you in here?!" she called out, but the house was silent, still filled with the stench of gas from the stove.

"Sara!" she yelled again. She stepped back outside and looked towards the field and the pond. She glanced around the yard but couldn't see Sara anywhere. She ran around the side of the house, to the front yard.

"Sara! Where are you?!" she called out, starting to panic, as her mind began to shuffle through the possibilities of where Sara could be. She ran back to the backyard and started searching by the pool. She looked out towards the field and still couldn't see Sara. The wooden pier was empty and she began to run towards the pond.

"Sara!" she called out, but still no reply came as the anxiety began to build inside of her.

Claire could feel her heart beating faster and her mind racing with fear as she searched the grounds for Sara. When she couldn't find her anywhere, she ran back inside the house and up the stairs calling for her, but still nothing. Sara was nowhere to be found.

Frantically, Claire picked up the phone to call the Sheriff's office. "Sheriff, this is Claire Cole out at 766 U.S. 61. My daughter Sara is missing. She was just outside and now she is gone. I can't find her anywhere!"

"Calm down, ma'am," the sheriff said. "I'll send a deputy right away."

"Thank you! Hurry!" Claire said. As she hung up the phone, she quickly called Jason at work. "Jason!" she started sobbing almost unable to catch her breath. "Jason, she's gone! I can't find her anywhere!"

"Claire? Calm down. Who is gone? What are you talking about?" Jason said.

"It's Sara! The house was full of gas when we got home and I told her to stand outside. It was just a few minutes and I can't find her anywhere. I looked everywhere," Claire replied, sobbing into the phone as she sat on the floor in her living room. "She just vanished!"

"Claire! She has to be there somewhere. I'm on my way. Did you look in the field? She didn't get near the pond, did she?" Jason started to grab his things and run towards his truck.

"No. I mean I checked the pond, the pool, the house. Nothing," Claire sobbed. She started to look around the house again.

"The field! Claire, check the field!" Jason said. "I'm on my way!"

Claire hung the phone up and ran out the back door towards the field calling for Sara. The wind was blowing and she took another look at the pond but the water was still without so much as a ripple. She ran towards the field but she couldn't find Sara anywhere.

After a while Claire heard the sound of the Sheriff's car pull up in front of the house and she ran back to meet him.

As the sheriff's deputy stepped out of the car, he walked towards Claire who was running up to him crying hysterically.

"Calm down, ma'am," the deputy said. "It's going to be okay. Why don't you take a deep breath and tell me what happened?"

Claire explained everything she could to the deputy. He walked back to his car and called someone on his radio. Stepping back out he looked at Claire and said, "Let's take another look, I'm sure she is here somewhere. It's a big yard, maybe she just ran off playing."

They both walked through the house first looking through every room. "Why is this door nailed shut?" the deputy asked, referring to the attic.

"Oh, it's nothing," Claire said, as she started to walk back down the stairs. "She can't even get in there. I think we should look outside."

"Ma'am, I'm going to need to look inside this room," the deputy said, looking more sternly at Claire than he had before.

"What? No, she can't even get in there. We're wasting time!" Claire said frustratedly as she continued to go down the stairs.

"Mrs. Cole," the deputy called. "You want to bring me a hammer, so I can take these nails out?"

"You're not listening," Claire said, as she stopped and looked up the stairs at the deputy. "She isn't in that room!"

"I'm not going to ask again," the deputy said, staring down at Claire with a stern look on his face. "Bring me something to un-nail this door or I'm breaking it down."

Claire shook her head frustrated, took a deep breath and went to get the hammer out of the drawer. She handed it to the deputy, shaking her head as tears ran down her face. "She can't get in there," she said, letting out a deep breath.

The deputy un-nailed the door, opened it up and stepped into the attic, turning on the light and looking around at all the boxes scattered about on the floor. The attic smelled musty and he walked over and looked out the window and into the back yard.

"Why was this door nailed shut?" he asked Claire, looking back towards her.

"Because... it opens, and I didn't want it to," Claire said, wiping her eyes. "Please. Help me find my daughter!"

The deputy took another look around the attic and then noticed the small door. He walked over to it and opened it up. He shinned his light into the small room. It was filled with insulation. He closed the small door back and turned the attic light off as he stepped back into the game room and shut the attic door behind him. They continued to look through every room in the house. Every closet, under every bed and behind every door. Still they couldn't find any trace of Sara in the house.

They walked outside and began to search around the pool and as they walked towards the pond, Claire heard another car pull into the driveway. It was Jason, he came running around the side of the house.

"Claire!" he called out frantically.

"Jason!" Claire ran towards Jason and he hugged her tight as she began to cry again.

"I can't find her!" sobbed Claire as she clung to Jason's chest.

"It's okay," Jason said looking at Claire. "We'll find her."

"Deputy, I'm Jason Cole, the father," Jason said, as he walked up to the deputy who had just stepped onto the wooden pier over the pond.

"Mr. Cole," the deputy said, shaking Jason's hand. "I think we should search the field. I don't think she fell into the pond, or... we would know by now."

Claire looked up at the deputy and then back at Jason. They all began to call out Sara's name as they walked through the fields looking for her. Suddenly, Jason heard a dog barking in the distance and he stopped abruptly.

"Did you hear that?" he asked Claire.

"What?" Claire said as they pushed their way through the fields.

"I thought I heard a..." Jason was interrupted by Claire screaming, "Sara!"

As they ran to the edge of the field, they could see Sara standing still, her white dress covered with dirt as she stared emptily out into the field.

"What are you doing out here?! Didn't you hear me calling you?!" Claire said wrapping her arms around Sara and picking her up. "Sara? Are you okay?"

Sara said nothing and looked as if she was in shock.

"Sara, are you okay?" Jason asked putting his hand on her head.

The deputy walked over to them, "Well, thank God. I'm glad we found her."

"Thank you," Jason said, reaching out and shaking the deputy's hand. "It was quite the scare."

They all walked back towards the house and Sara said nothing at all as she clung tightly to Claire's neck.

As the deputy got into his car and drove away, Jason looked at Sara, "You gave us quite a scare. Come here." He took Sara from Claire and sat down on the porch with her on his lap. "What happened to you?" he asked. Sara said nothing and just stared at Jason. "Sara, what were you doing in the field?" he asked again.

"How did you get dirty? Why did you move? I told you to stay there," Claire said, wiping Sara's face. "You scared us, so bad. Why didn't you answer me? Sara?"

But Sara said nothing and just stared at Claire and Jason.

"Come on, I'll get you cleaned up," Claire took Sara inside the house and walked upstairs to her bathroom.

Sara was quiet the rest of the night and after dinner she finally said, "Daddy, I was looking for you."

"What?" Jason asked.

"In the field, I... I thought I saw you. And then, there was a..." Sara began to tear up.

"Hey, it's okay," Jason said, putting his hand on Sara's back. "You just got lost. I'm here. Everything is okay." He got up and hugged her tight. "How about I read you a story tonight before bed?"

Sara nodded, "Okay."

"Well, I'm going to take a bath myself," Claire said, exhausted from the day. "I'm just emotionally drained from everything."

Jason carried Sara upstairs to read her a story and put her to bed while Claire cleaned up after dinner before going to soak in a hot bath. She had forgotten all about Gabriel, Father Taylor and even the bookstore. Emotionally, she was a complete wreck, and she couldn't think of anything past a hot bath.

* * *

AFTER A WHILE, Jason came downstairs and found Claire lying in the bed staring up at the ceiling. He climbed into bed next to her and held her in his arms.

"I don't think I have ever been that scared in my life," Claire said, looking over at Jason. "Well maybe the pond thing."

Jason started to stroke Claire hair, "It's okay, Sara was pretty shaken up. I doubt she will ever go towards the field alone again. She must have just got turned around."

"Did she say anything else?" Claire asked, sitting up in bed.

"No, and I didn't want to push her. She was really upset, and whatever happened she didn't want to talk about it."

"Longest day ever," Claire said, and she lay back down with Jason. "I feel like I'm losing my mind." Suddenly she remembered Pastor Gabriel and their conversation and she looked back at Jason, "I stopped by the church today to speak with Gabriel and apparently he found something out. His friend, Father Taylor from the French Quarters wants to come here and have a look around and talk to us himself. Gabriel said he thinks he can help. They will be here tomorrow night."

"The priest?" Jason asked, looking curiously at Claire. "This is almost like a bad joke. A priest and a pastor go into a haunted house with two crazy people, and no one comes out!"

"Jason, maybe they will help. Something has to give. I don't think I can take any more." She rolled over and put her head on Jason's chest.

"It's going to be okay, I promise," Jason said, stroking her hair.

"That's what everyone keeps telling me," Claire closed her eyes.

After a while, they both fell asleep, lying there thinking of all the possibilities of what could be happening.

* * *

THE HOUSE WAS QUIET, except for the clinking of the wind
chimes, blowing in the wind, on the front porch. A dark shadow
was moving through the house, room to room, as Jason and
Claire slept soundly in their bed. Their door slowly opened and
the demon moved inside their room. Its heavy breathing
pierced through the silence and the floors creaked beneath its
footsteps, until it stopped next to Jason's side of the bed. It was
staring down at him with its piercing red eyes, then it moved its
hand on top of Jason's chest. His breathing became erratic and
the demon looked upward as its mouth elongated, and thousands of whispers filled the room. Claire rolled over to the
other side of the bed clutching her pillow tightly as she slept but
Jason became more and more restless and he began to dream.

*HE COULD SEE himself lying on the bed and the demon standing
over him, however he couldn't move. As the demon looked down at
him through its hollow dark eyes, it grinned wickedly as Jason
struggled to free himself from what felt like a ton of bricks
weighing down on his chest. Jason looked towards Claire, who he
could see sleeping undisturbed next to him in bed. His pulse raced
as he struggled to catch his breath. He closed his eyes to avoid
looking up at the demon standing over him, though he could smell
the stench in the air of a dead animal. He felt sickened at his
stomach and fear overtook every part of his body. The demon took
its other hand and with its long, tarnished nails, it pried Jason's
eyelids open. He could feel the nails piercing through the skin
above his eyes and feared it would jab its nails into his eyes at any
moment. "See," the demon whispered, and all of a sudden Jason
could see himself standing in the living room and Sara dressed in
her pink nightgown standing still at the bottom of the stairs. The
house was dark except for the moonlight shining through an open*

window and the curtains blowing in the cool breeze of the night air. "Sara!" Jason called out, but Sara didn't move. He could still feel the sharp piercing pain going through the skin around his eyes as the demon pressed its nails farther in. Sara's long blonde hair blowing back as she stood frozen, staring at Jason. He tried to move towards her but his feet felt glued to the spot on the floor and he could still feel the heavy weight upon his chest. "Sara!" he called out again. Then he noticed the shadowy figure of a woman, in what appeared to be a long flowing dress, with dark black hair and haunting blue eyes, standing at the top of the stairs behind Sara. Jason knew he had seen her before. She opened her mouth and let out an eerie screech. Sara's head tilted up and her eyes rolled back. Her mouth dropped open and blood dripped from her lips as she began to convulse. Jason's eye's widened with fear and he tried to scream. He could see blood pouring slowly down the walls around the stairway. The thick red liquid running down each step, one at a time, closer and closer to Sara. His mind raced as he tried to free himself from the demon's hold. The back door flew open and Jason could see something else, out of the corner of his eye, standing in the doorway. It moved in the house and stepped towards Sara. Its hooves hit the wooden floor one step at a time and the house echoed with the sound of its pounding feet. It reached Sara and turned back and looked directly at Jason. It was something Jason had not seen before. It was tall and big and had the body of a man but the head of a bull. Eyes that were black and hollow, black horns and distorted hands with long razor-like nails. It looked back at Sara who was still standing, eyes rolled back in her head, blood dripping from her lips and eyes and with a voice that sounded like rushing water it spoke, "She belongs to me." Jason's body shook while he struggled to breathe and as the beast turned towards him, it struck its sharp nails across Jason's throat and his flesh and blood oozed out.

. . .

JASON AWOKE SCREAMING, covered with sweat. He started coughing and gagging and ran to the bathroom, fell upon the floor by the commode and started to throw up. He could still smell the stench of the dead animal and his stomach was weak from the odor that seem to linger in the air. He sat on the floor for a few minutes to catch his breath and then got up, looked in the mirror and splashed some cold water over his face. He stood there staring in the mirror for a few minutes trying to process the dream in his mind. The picture of the beast that was now burned into his thoughts, haunted him endlessly. He suddenly thought about Sara. He wiped his face and looked at Claire, still somehow lying sound asleep in bed. He began to leave the room and check on Sara when a loud banging came from the attic, above their bedroom. Claire awoke from a sound sleep. "Jason!" she called out.

He stepped quickly back into the room. "It's okay, I'm right here," he said.

"Did you hear that?" Claire asked, listening again for the noise.

"Yes," answered Jason. "I heard it."

Something hit the window outside of their bedroom with a loud bang.

"Jason!" Claire screamed as she jumped out of bed and moved away from the window. Their bedroom door slammed shut with both of them standing inside the room. Jason reached for the doorknob and tried to open it, but it wouldn't budge.

"Jason! Sara!" Claire cried. All of the sudden heavy footsteps and deep breathing echoed throughout their bedroom. Claire held tightly to Jason's arm as he struggled to try and open the bedroom door.

With a final jerk of the door, it opened, and all at once, all of the lights went out and the house fell silent. Jason looked at Claire and they both ran up the stairs to Sara's room. The bedroom door was open but Sara wasn't in her bed. Claire began to panic as they started to run through the upstairs looking for Sara who was nowhere to be found.

"Sara!" Claire screamed out. "Sara! Where are you?!"

"Sara!" Jason called out as he ran back down the stairs searching the house.

As Claire ran back down the stairs, she noticed the back door wide open.

"Jason!" Claire screamed. "The back door!"

Jason quickly came into the room and they both ran outside yelling for Sara.

"Sara!" Claire called, her mind racing in a shear panic. All she could think of was Sara, the day before, standing in the field covered with dirt, in a state of shock. "Sara!" she screamed out.

"Sara!" Jason yelled, as visions of the beast from his night-mare, kept flashing through his mind.

Claire ran as fast as she could, straight for the field, as a thick fog rolled in off the bayou and filled the night air. Jason not far behind her, noticed a slight ripple in the pool water and stopped and looked down into the swimming pool. "Sara!" Jason called out, as he stood at the edge of the pool looking down into the water, when suddenly a hand with rotten flesh reached up out of the water and grabbed Jason's ankle and jerked him into the pool. As it pulled him deeper down into the water towards the bottom, Jason could see a black figure swimming towards him. He tried to struggle to free himself but the hand held him firmly and he could not escape its grip.

Claire reached the edge of the field but the fog was so thick she could hardly see through it.

"Sara!" she called out, frantically looking around her when she noticed Jason was nowhere in sight. "Jason!" Claire yelled, and she started running through the field from side to side but she could see no one; only the heavy fog rolling through the night air and a black crow that almost hit her as it flew by with a loud caw.

As Jason struggled to try and pull himself up out of the water, the dark figure came closer to him and he feared he would not be able to hold his breath much longer. As it stood in front of him in the water it cocked its head and reached for Jason's throat, wrapping its long fingers around Jason's neck and squeezing tightly. It was all Jason could do to try and hold on and not gasp for air as he tried to pull its hand off of his throat.

Claire heard the splashing coming from the pool and quickly ran back towards it.

"Sara! Jason!" she screamed out, as she reached the edge of the pool.

She could see Jason struggling in the water, at the bottom of the pool but couldn't see anything holding him down. She jumped in the pool and grabbed hold of Jason's arm and yanked him up towards the top. Jason opened his eyes, gasping for air as he came up out of the deep blue water.

"Jason!" Claire cried. "Are you okay?" She searched the water again to see if she could see any signs of Sara but she was nowhere to be found. She helped pull Jason to the edge of the pool and they both pulled themselves up out of the water. Jason collapsed on the deck to catch his breath and Claire jumped to her feet and ran towards the pond.

"Sara!" she yelled out again, as she reached the wooden pier and looked down into the murky water. She could feel the chill of the night air blowing through her wet clothes and she fell to her knees exhausted, as tears began to run down her face. Her eyes frantically searched the surface of the pond for any signs of Sara.

Jason pulled himself up and looking back at the water he could see a pair of red eyes staring up at him, from deep in the pool. He moved backwards, unable to blink or take his eyes away from the thing he could still see in the bottom of the pool, then turned quickly and ran towards Claire and the pond.

"Sara!" Jason called, as he looked around the yard, still dripping wet and trying to focus his thoughts. He bent over and held his throat for a moment, which still felt sore from the grip of the demon in the pool.

When Claire looked back and saw Jason, she took a deep breath and forced herself to get up. She knew she had to keep going and find Sara. She ran to Jason and wrapped her arms around him. "Are you okay?" she asked. "What happened? Jason, where's Sara?" she cried.

Still bending over, feeling sick at his stomach, he thought he might throw up again. "We'll find her," he said. As he looked at Claire standing beside him, he could see the fear in her eyes and he knew he had to pull it together for her sake and for Sara. Just then he noticed a light coming from the small wooden shack near the pond.

"Claire, the shack!' cried Jason, and they both ran towards it.

As they reached the door, Jason jerked on the knob, but it wouldn't open.

"It's stuck!" Jason said as he tried to pull harder. "Sara!" he called out, as he beat on the door with his fist.

"Sara!" Claire screamed, "Are you in there?" She tried to pull on the knob again but the door wouldn't budge.

Jason ran back towards the house and grabbed an axe that was on the side of the house and ran back to the shack and started hitting the doorknob with the axe until it broke. As they pushed the door open, out of the dark came a swarm of flies and the smell of decaying flesh filled the air.

"Sara!" screamed Claire frantically.

They could see Sara lying on the floor inside of the shack, in front of a what appeared to be a large glass case. She had stones circling around her and Claire knew in an instant, she had seen all of this before. The bookstore... Jason's eyes widened big as he looked at what was sitting inside the case and fear filled every part of his body.

It was a statue of the beast just like Jason had seen in his dream, just like Claire had seen in the bookstore. Its black eyes seem to stare through the case directly at Jason. Sara lie on the wooden floor in front of the case not moving. Claire ran towards her, coughing from the smell and covering her mouth with her hand as she grabbed Sara up in her arms, kicking the stones out of the way.

"Claire. Get Sara out of here now," Jason said, as a chill ran through his entire body. He was trying not to gag from the stench. Claire picked up Sara and ran out of the shack and back towards the house until her body could take no more and she collapsed down in the grass holding Sara close. "Sara!" she cried out. "Sara, wake up. Please!" Sara lay in her arms, her eyes closed with no response.

Jason looked at the case, and then noticed a gas canister in the corner. He grabbed it and started pouring gas all around the shed and splashing it on the case.

"No!" he yelled out. "You can't have her!" He ran out of the shed, towards the house, through the back door and into the kitchen searching for matches or a lighter. Claire sat on the ground crying, holding Sara in her arms, still trying to wake her.

As Jason reached inside the kitchen drawer, he felt the matches, grabbed them and ran back to the shed. He lit the match and threw it into the shed and the gasoline immediately caught fire. A loud boom echoed through the night as the wooden shack blew up, knocking Jason back onto the ground.

Suddenly Sara opened her eyes, "Mommy?" she called out, looking up at Claire.

"Sara!" cried Claire, hugging her tightly to her chest as she let out a sigh of relief.

Jason ran over to them and fell upon the ground and wrapped his arms around both of them. They tried to catch their breath and calm down as they watched the shed burn down to the ground.

"Mom?" Sara rubbed her eyes. "What are we doing outside?" She seemed to have no memory of the night at all. Jason picked her up and helped Claire off the ground and they walked back inside the house and the shed became a distant glow in the night.

As they went back inside, Claire took Sara into their bathroom to clean her up. As she wiped away the dirt from Sara's arms and legs, she felt complete exhaustion take over her once again. As if she had no more energy left in her to so much as take another step let alone take a shower herself. Her head was hammering out a terrible headache and she felt sick at her stomach. She used every bit of strength she had to finish bathing Sara, dress her and put her in their bed. As she stepped into the shower and turned it on, she felt her knees buckle as she dropped down, sitting on the ceramic tiles of the shower. While the hot water rushed over her, she broke down into tears. She stayed in there for almost an hour sobbing, before Jason stepped into the bathroom, took off his clothes and got into the shower with her. Picking her up off the shower floor, he held her in his arms.

"It's over," he said, running his hands through Claire's hair and trying to comfort her. "It's over."

They said nothing more and finally after they were dressed, they were able to crawl into bed with Sara and try and put the night out of their minds. They listened close to every sound in the house as they drifted off to sleep but they heard nothing else. The house was quiet.

ASHES OF PEACE

he next morning, Jason got out of bed and looked out the bedroom window at what was left of the shed next to the pond. It had burned down to nothing but a pile of ashes through the night. He couldn't believe everything they had been through since they moved into the house. He wished more than anything that he had never moved them there. "What was I thinking? This town has been nothing but horrible since the accident. This is my fault we're here."

Just then Claire woke up and looked at Jason. She could tell he was deep in thought and was worried about him. She got out of bed and wrapped her arms around him.

"Hey, whatcha thinking about?" she asked. "Or do I want to know?" she said with a slight grin.

'I'm sorry, Claire," Jason said looking down and shaking his head. "I should have never brought us here."

"Hey," Claire put her hands on Jason's face and gently forced him to look at her. "We're okay. I love you. I'm always going to be beside you no matter what happens. If it's here or anywhere else, I would follow you anywhere."

Jason looked at her and kissed her as tears rolled down his face, "I love you too."

Just then Sara began to stir awake and she rolled over in bed looking at Jason and Claire.

"Can we get pizza?" she asked wiping her eyes and stretching out.

Claire and Jason looked at each other and laughed.

"Today, we can get anything you want," Jason said as he reached down and picked her up off the bed.

"Pizza at 9 in the morning," Claire smirked.

"Well, for lunch then," Jason winked at Sara and then leaned over and kissed her on the forehead. "I'll even let you pick out a book from bookstore."

"No!" Claire said turning around with a quick jerk.

"What?" Jason looked at Claire confused.

"No, just… How about a toy from the toy store instead?" Claire asked. "She has plenty of books."

Claire still didn't want Jason to know anything about the bookstore. He was feeling bad enough as it was and she didn't want to add anything more to their long night.

He looked at Claire with a questioning look on his face and shook his head, "Toy it is. But first, how about we lie in bed and watch a movie together. I think the day can wait," he crawled back into bed and held Sara close to him.

"How about I fix us some pancakes first," Claire said.

"Yay!" Sara yelled, as she snuggled up next to Jason.

Claire went into the kitchen to make pancakes. She still felt emotionally drained from the night even though she did have a sense of relief that they had finally found what they were looking for in the house and gotten rid of it. "How could Charlotte have had that thing out there?" she thought. "Like some sort of altar. What was she thinking and how much of it had to do with Kristina?" Claire didn't want to go to the bookstore anymore or have anything to do with Kristina

Graves. She wanted to distance herself as far from her as she could.

As Jason lay in bed with Sara, they put on a movie and his mind began to wander again. "What was that thing out in the shed and why did grandmother have it out there? Maybe she didn't even know it was there? Maybe someone put it there and that's why she had the bolt on her door." Flashes of the night kept going through his mind, no matter how hard he tried not to think of it.

Just then Claire came in the room with two plates of hot pancakes for Jason and Sara and set them on a tray. She handed Jason his plate and as he poured the syrup over his pancakes, his thoughts went back to flashes of the blood running slowly down the stairs around Sara in his dream.

"Jason," Claire said, as the syrup began to run off his plate and drip onto the bed.

"Oh shit, I'm sorry Claire," Jason grabbed a hand towel and wiped the syrup off the sheet. "I was just..."

"It's okay," Claire interrupted, gently taking the towel from Jason and smiling at him as she threw it in the hamper.

"I'm sorry," he said, and he reached for her hand.

"I understand," Claire said. "Me too. I just... don't want to talk about any of it."

"Agreed." He kissed her hand.

Claire stepped out, grabbed her plate and then came back in the bedroom and crawled into bed next to Sara. They all finished up their breakfast without saying much of anything else. Afterwards, they lay in bed watching the movie, glimpses of the night haunting their thoughts as they stared emptily at the television. Sara seemed to be the only one truly enjoying the morning with no memories of the night before, as Jason and Claire went through the motions, numb to everything around them until they both drifted off back to sleep. It was the best sleep they had both had in a long time.

* * *

LATER THAT AFTERNOON when they awoke from their long day of sleep, they got up and dressed to go into town. The house was quiet and they didn't talk to each other much. They didn't have much to say after the night before. The memories kept playing on a loop in their minds, taunting them back to the field behind the house.

"Are you ready?" Claire asked, looking at Jason still gathering himself and pulling a t-shirt over his head.

"Sure," he grabbed his shoes from the closet.

They gathered up Sara and loaded into the car to head into town. Jason wanted to keep Sara out of it as much as possible, so they avoided talking about any of it around her.

"Why don't you take Sara for that toy you promised her and I'll walk over to the church and see if I can catch Gabriel and find out what time they are coming by the house tonight?" Claire said. "We don't want anything else to happen."

Jason agreed and they pulled the car into the parking lot at the end of Main Street where everyone usually parked to walk through the town's main shops.

"Let's go, Sara," Jason said, acting excited for Sara's sake. Inside his mind, flashes of her covered with blood, standing at the bottom of the stairs, kept playing repeatedly when he looked at her.

"Okay Daddy!" Sara said enthusiastically. She was already running the toy store through her mind as to which toy would be the lucky winner that came home with her today.

As they reached the store, Sara pushed passed Jason and headed straight for the dolls.

They were lined on the shelves in rows of boxes filled with every kind of doll a little girl could want. Sara carefully eyed each doll as the potential winner and one by one she worked her way through the end of the aisle. "Nope!" she said finally. "None of these. Let's look at Barbies!"

Jason watched her as she turned down the next aisle filled with Barbie dolls. "The innocence of a child must be nice," he thought. "Nothing to worry about except which toy to pick out. Those were the days." They continued up and down each aisle as Sara carefully weighed her options for which toy would be the best one to take home.

* * *

CLAIRE WALKED down the street looking at all the shops. A gentle breeze blew her hair back and she could feel the sun shining down on her skin. The day seemed like a perfectly beautiful sunny afternoon, but she knew the truth behind the birds chirping in the trees. She knew what the night held. As she reached the church, she could see Pastor Gabriel standing outside watering the flowers.

"Pastor," she called out. "Hello."

Gabriel reached over and turned the water off and put the hose down.

"Claire," he said, as he walked towards her. "Are you okay?"

He took Claire's hand and gave it a firm but soft shake. "Is everything alright at the house?"

Claire walked inside with Gabriel and told him everything that had happened the night before with the shed and the terrible thing they saw sitting inside the case. As Gabriel listened to all the horrific details that took place, he poured Claire a glass of water while she tried to catch her breath.

"It was the worst thing I've ever been through," Claire said. "Even more than the day my dad stepped into my room to tell me my mom wasn't coming home." That was a day that was burned into Claire's memory from her childhood. Even though she was only three she could still recall the smell of apple pie baking in the kitchen, when her father came in to talk to her that cold winter afternoon. To this day Claire couldn't stand the smell of apple pie.

"Claire," Gabriel said, sitting down next to her. "I'm afraid whatever was in your house might still be there." He looked at her as she wiped away her tears.

"What?" She asked. "But we burned it down?"

"I'm sorry Claire," Gabriel started, "but chances are whatever was lurking in your house... it's still there. What you burned down sounds more like an offering altar. Evil altars empower demons and give them access to your family. Often, they call for a blood sacrifice to honor some kind of agreement or to give power to a covenant of some sort. It can be used to control the destinies for generations of whomever it chooses. You did good in destroying the altar but I'm afraid that wouldn't get rid of the demon that is already in your house. With all of the symbols you found, I'm afraid there is more. I'm sorry. I know that's not what you want to hear. Father Taylor will be down this after-noon. Claire, he knows what's going on in your house. He can help." He took hold of Claire's hand. "Hold onto your faith. I'm afraid there is a much bigger picture at play here than any of us could have imagined. We will come tonight around eight o'clock and Father Taylor will explain everything. The demon will be at its weakest with the altar burned down, and God willing, we'll banish that thing from your home for good."

"Thank you," Claire said, gripping Gabriel's hand tight.

"Be strong," he said. "We'll be there tonight."

Claire and Gabriel sat for another few minutes praying on the bench for strength to get them through what was yet to come.

As Claire left the church and was walking back down the street, she could see Jason and Sara step out of the toy store with a large blue bag.

"Mom!" Sara shouted. She spotted Claire down the street.

As Claire reached Jason and Sara, she bent down and hugged Sara tightly.

"I got a dolly," Sara said, excited as she pulled the box holding the doll out of the bag.

"It was the first one she looked at," smiled Jason. He noticed the look on Claire's face.

"What is it?" he asked.

"Nothing," Claire answered, but he could tell by the sound of her voice it was much more than nothing.

They walked in the pizza pub and sat down at one of the little tables by the window. As the waiter came over, they ordered their usual pizza with everything on it and one kids' cheese pizza for Sara. The smell of pizza sauce and cheese filled the air and was a welcoming aroma to all of them.

Claire looked at Jason, "I spoke to Gabriel."

"No," Jason said, quick to cut her off. "Please don't say anything to mess up the pizza coming."

"Jason," Claire started. "We still have a problem. Gabriel and Father Taylor are coming tonight."

"Dammit, Claire," Jason said, setting his glass of coke back on the table. "I asked you not to say anything." He took a deep breath and wiped his forehead.

"Jason, that's not going to magically make everything alright by me not saying it. It is what it is," Claire said. She reached over and took his hand.

"No. I guess not, but I could have enjoyed my pizza more not knowing," Jason held onto her hand. "When are they coming?"

"Around eight o'clock tonight." She took a deep breath. "They have to prepare, and after that, he said they will come."

"Okay," Jason said. "But anything more and we're moving and never looking back at this town again."

"Agreed," Claire said, nodding her head.

As the pizza finally found its way to their table, Jason and Claire dropped the subject and succumbed to listening to Sara as she took over the conversation introducing her new doll to the wonderful world of cheese pizza.

As they finished up and headed home, neither Claire nor Jason looked forward to what they knew awaited them that night. They drove past Old River Road and Jason looked out over the bridge thinking of his mother's accident.

Claire put her hand on Jason's shoulder, "Everything is going to be okay. We handled last night; we can handle anything."

Jason glanced back at Claire, "My mother's accident... I've thought a lot about it lately. The car and her body. Her face Claire, I never saw it but the doctors said she was unrecognizable. That wouldn't have happened from a drowning. She used to tell me something was following her and maybe if I just would have listened, things would have been different. Maybe I could have helped her somehow instead of being wrapped up in my own life. I just didn't listen. I should have gone with her that night she asked. I never even told her goodbye."

"Jason, no." Claire rubbed his shoulder. "What happened to Cindy, you couldn't have done anything. No one will ever know what really happened that night and your mom loved you. She wouldn't want you to blame yourself and no matter what it was, she was a God-loving woman and you know she is in heaven and at peace. Don't torture yourself anymore."

"I know, you're right," Jason said. "I just wonder if all this had something to do with her. If that thing or something like it, well, you know. She must have felt so scared and alone," he wiped a tear from his cheek.

"What are y'all talking about?" Sara asked, sitting forward in the backseat of the car.

"Nothing," Jason said, looking in the rearview mirror. "Put your seatbelt on and sit back."

Claire smiled at Jason. "Hopefully, after tonight it will all be over. If you decide you want us to move after this than I'm with you."

"No," Jason said. "We aren't being run out of our home, not again. That thing doesn't get to win."

They drove home and pulled into the driveway and Sara jumped out of the car and ran towards the house.

"For her," Jason said, looking at Claire, as they both stepped out of the car. "It doesn't get to win."

EXORCISM

Claire put Sara to bed early, and she and Jason spent some time sitting outside on the back patio.

"I haven't felt anything in the house since last night," Jason said, looking at Claire. "Are you sure it's not gone?"

"The pastor said it's probably regaining strength. I would rather be sure, besides, apparently Father Taylor knows more about it than we do," she replied.

"No, you're right," Jason fidgeted. "I just... I just want this to be over. I wanted a good life for us here and it's been nothing like I imagined."

"Hey, soon enough you will be sitting on the pier, fishing with Sara," Claire smiled. She rubbed his back with her hand as she glanced around the yard.

She seemed less fragile than Jason had remembered her from just a year ago. She had always been a strong woman but there was something different in her eyes now. She was not the same upbeat girl he remembered, waking up in the morning, singing silly songs she made up, while dressing Sara for the day. She was quieter, more withdrawn than he had ever seen her before. And even though she seemed fearless when it came to protecting Sara and facing the demon, she was jumpy and always looking around, checking over her shoulder to see if someone or something was there. Jason couldn't help but feel like even if they were able to rid their home of the demon, it had robbed them of their peace, and he prayed they would be able to get it back again.

Time seemed to go by slowly as the night grew darker and a light mist began to fall upon the ground. The wind picked up and a heavy fog rolled in off the bayou which filled the backyard.

"We better go inside," Jason said, picking up a cup as it started to blow off the patio.

They went in the house and closed everything up tight. It was just after 8:00 pm, and Claire began to wonder if Gabriel was still coming.

"I'm going to check on Sara," she said, as she started up the stairs.

Jason walked around downstairs, looking carefully in all the rooms. The house seemed almost too quiet except for the sound of the wind howling through the trees and the wind-chimes blowing on the front porch. All of the sudden Jason heard a loud noise. Bang! He jumped back into the wall and looked towards the front door. Bang! The sound came again and Jason walked slowly towards the window and peered out the curtain. He let out a sigh of relief when he noticed it was just the front porch swing blowing up against the house. Claire wasn't the only one that had changed since they moved back. Jason had become quite jumpy himself.

As Claire opened Sara's door slowly, she walked into her room and started to pick the toys up from off the floor and put them in the toy box. She sat next to Sara on the bed and started to stroke her hair. The dragonfly had fallen on the floor again and she picked it up and put it on the shelf.

A creaking sound came from down the hall and Claire turned her head slowly towards Sara's bedroom door.

"Jason?" Claire called out softly.

She got up and slowly walked across Sara's room listening carefully. She opened the door and looked at the last bedroom towards the end of the hallway. The door was half open. She glanced back at Sara and slowly walked down the hall towards the room, staring at the open door. Her hand was trembling as she reached out to grab the door knob and pull the door shut. She stood there for a moment trying to remember if the door was open or not when she first went upstairs. The doorbell rang and she jumped back against the wall. She walked back down the stairs and as she reached the bottom, the bedroom door slowly creaked open again. Pastor Gabriel was shaking hands with Jason and introducing Father Taylor as they stepped inside the house.

"Good evening," the pastor said, looking at Claire. "This is Father Taylor." He looked back at the priest. "And this... is Claire."

"Gabriel, I'm so glad you're here. Father Taylor, we can't thank you enough for coming," she said, as she took Jason's hand and held it tightly for a moment.

Jason stood looking at both the pastor and the priest and the joke he thought of the other day crept back into his mind for just a moment. "Father Taylor so nice to meet you. I wish it was under better circumstances. We can't tell you both how much we really appreciate you being here. It's been a nightmare."

Father Taylor looked around the house as they walked into the living room and took a seat on the sofa. "I'm not sure where to begin, so I'll start from the beginning. Gabriel tells me you have seen the demon in your dreams?"

"Yes," Jason said, looking down. "It clawed me. I still have the marks on my neck." He pulled his shirt aside to reveal red streaks on his throat.

"And the hound?" Taylor asked. "Is it during your sleep or when you're awake?"

"We haven't had any problems with dogs or hounds. It's just doors opening and closing and stomping and... it constantly attacks us when we are asleep. What does it want? We destroyed some case in the shed," Claire said. She shook her head as tears filled her eyes and she tried to wipe them away before anyone noticed.

"Actually," Jason interrupted. He glanced at Claire before he looked back at the priest. "I have seen the dog or a dog; a big black Rottweiler. First in my dream and then, everywhere I look, it seems to be there, staring at me with these black eyes."

Claire looked at Jason in surprise, "You never told me anything about a dog?"

"Claire, there has been so much going," he grabbed hold of her hand.

"Okay," she looked back at Father Taylor. "I stand corrected, apparently we have a dog thing too."

Father Taylor reached in his bag and pulled out a prayer shawl, a cross and a container full of holy water and a bible and placed them all on the coffee table in front of them as he started to speak. "A long time ago when I was a young man, there was a girl where I lived who suffered a great many things as you have here. She was involved in the dark arts and so I believed at the time, that was drawing the things to her. I left town to go to the Vatican to see what I could learn and when I returned, she had changed. She grew darker than before and I started to research all that I had learned while I was away. The arch bishops in the Vatican were well aware of her story and what was happening. They gave me all the information I needed to stop it and I've been searching for the demon ever since. There were others besides the girl in the Quarter... Four other girls to be exact over the course of the years. An evil spirit known as the Hell Witch. She visited everyone that was involved in these series of attacks." He took a breath as he opened the bible and sprinkled the holy water on the cross. "Mr. and Mrs. Cole, I'm afraid what she is after isn't either of you at all." He pulled out another book and opened it up to a picture of a woman. "This is Eva Horne, better known now as the Hell Witch. She was a powerful sorcerer in her time, actually in this town." He turned the page to an old picture of St. Francisville. She was burned alive in these fields behind your house. The men in town, six of them came and attacked her in the middle of the night. She was married and had a little girl about six years old, Emma was her name. It is one of this town's darkest secrets." He turned the page in the book to a group of six men. "These men... killed her husband first, slit his throat and he bled out in the field. The little girl..." he stopped and took a deep breath. "The child... they never did find. Eva was dragged from her home and burned in the middle of the field next to her husband."

"Who are these men?" Jason pointed to a picture tucked into the book.

"You must understand. This can go no farther than this room. I'm only telling you this because it's important for you to understand what we are dealing with. Jason, the Vatican ordered it be done. She was practicing evil beyond what you could possibly understand. She had to be stopped. She was conjuring up demons. The girl... it was unfortunate that she was caught up in it."

"Wait! You're telling me all of this is happening to us because a group of priests decided to have a witch burned in our back-yard?!" Jason stood up, glaring at the two men.

"Jason, please," Claire begged. "What do we do now?"

Jason sat back down, rubbing his head. "So what does this have to do with us? Wrong house?"

"Jason, please let me continue," Father Taylor said. "The men in the photograph. They were head of the town council at the time." He began to point to them one by one. "This is Ben

Thompson, this Ademola Graves, this man in the hat is Ken Richards. This is Mike Peterson standing next to Charles Kingston and this... this is Robert Cole."

"Robert Cole?" Jason looked at Gabriel, puzzled.

"Jason, he is your great, great grandfather," Gabriel said.

"Perfect!" Jason exclaimed. "So some evil witch is seeking revenge? What the hell does any of this have to do with us?!"

"Jason, please. Father Taylor, go on," Claire grabbed Jason's hand as the priest continued to turn the page.

"Eva practiced a very dark art. Some think she killed her daughter herself, to protect her from the men that were coming back. We believe she made a pact with the devil himself to resurrect her daughter at some point in the future and in return she is releasing six demons."

"The symbols!" Claire jumped up and reached in the drawer to grab the pictures she had taken of the shed. She handed them to father Taylor. "I tried to figure out what these were but I could only find a match for one of the symbols. They were on the shed." She stopped abruptly and looked back at Jason. "The Petersons' hardware store. Mike Peterson!" She looked at Gabriel, "Ademola Graves. Kristina? They are all connected."

"The symbols represent a powerful spell. The pact she made before she was killed." Father Taylor turned to a page marked with the symbols and began to point them out one by one. "These markings represent a release of six demons on the earth. With them will come great sickness and destruction. They each will carry with them an evil that will spread once it is released. All five will bring great devastation and when the sixth demon is released." He pointed to the final symbol. "Resurrection. With this demon, we believe it will release the Hell Witch herself and resurrect her daughter. The demons will be set loose on the earth forever, pouring out the evil they brought with them."

"She's trying to bring back her daughter," Claire said. "Father. In the attic, before, I saw a child. Only for a few minutes. At first it was bones in the middle of a circle of stones. Then it was a young girl lying in the circle. It vanished right after. We found Sara, when she was lost. We found her in the shed. She was lying in the middle of a circle of stones, in front of a statue of a beast of some sort. You said she isn't after us. She wants Sara?"

"Hold on, please. There is more," Taylor said. "The girls have been chosen as they are descendants of the men. She is trading their souls to the beast to release the demons. Pulling them into darkness to spread evil until the final girl is taken. One by one she has been cultivating them. Sara is the last girl but she will not try and take her just yet. She is marking her for later." He stood up and looked towards the stairs. "There is always a blood sacrifice, someone the girl loves. She needs it to turn their heart completely dark. Every girl was consumed by evil after the sacrifice was complete. All five of the girls were sixteen when it happened. It comes to them from an early age to pull them into darkness slowly and then it uses them when the time comes. The Vatican has been tracking the demons release for some time. After each sacrifice is complete and the darkness takes the girl, an evil breaks out around her and the demons seek out the next girl with the calling. In my day, it was the French Quarter that held the demon. Violence broke out into the streets unlike anything I've ever seen before and we believe the red-eyed demon was released by the young girl there at the time. A few short years from that another girl from right here in this town, went through the same thing and disease and illness took over the town and killed many people. We believe the yellow-eyed demon was released by her at that time. To date five demons have been released into the world, each carrying their own form of destruction. The green-eyed demon released in Kinder brought about lust, the orange-eyed demon in the back bayou released from a young girl who killed her parents shortly after. We believe that demon released the hounds that you see. They will kill you if they catch you."

Father Taylor started to walk around the room, sprinkling holy water around as he continued. "The dark figure with blue eyes. You have no doubt, seen her, the Hell Witch. She is the most dangerous of all and controls the demons until the final release. We believe she's gaining strength to release the sixth and final one. The white-eyed demon of resurrection," he looked at Jason. "I believe your daughter Sara is the last calling to release the final demon. When she does finally come for her, and she will try. We believe with the resurrection, the girls will all die."

Jason stood up and looked at the priest. "No," he said, shaking his head. "This can't be happening. Why, I mean? She is just a child. This can't be true. She is innocent, not dark. We don't have anything to do with all of this."

Father Taylor walked over to Jason. "They were all children, early in age when she first appeared to them. These girls were chosen, seduced by the darkness to spread evil. All descendants of the men that killed Eva Horne. Jason, the Hell Witch cannot be allowed to release the last demon. If she succeeds, not only will all the girls die but the world will suffer greatly and all the demons will be free to spread their destruction endlessly throughout the earth. There will be no stopping them once the white-eyed demon comes. We need to save your daughter but we have to stop the Hell Witch at all costs. She is marking her now but she will return for her when she is sixteen."

"Why the dreams?" Claire asked, looking at Father Taylor. "Sara is barely affected by the demon at all and none of us have seen this witch you're talking about."

Father Taylor continued to sprinkle the holy water on the cross and looked at Claire. "The demons attack you to distract you from their real purpose. They are tormenting creatures by nature and have the most advantage over you while you are asleep and your soul is at rest. Depending on their strength they can be quite dangerous. No doubt they have been visiting your daughter Sara, as well. Perhaps they come to her in a different form to prep her for what is to come later on. She is the last child to release the final demon. They will stop at nothing to reach her even if it means killing everyone around her. The beast is quite crafty and should not be taken lightly. He has no doubt been deciding who will stand in his way and who can be swayed and used to his advantage. I myself have had several close calls but my faith in God is strong and the beast is not stronger than Him."

Jason looked at Father Taylor again. "What does this Hell Witch look like?"

The priest looked back at Jason, as if he knew what he was thinking. "She comes in different forms, mostly a beautiful woman with long black hair and wretched blue eyes, but make no mistake she is centered with the beast and pure evil."

Claire looked at Jason curiously, but he wouldn't look her in the eye for the feeling of guilt from his dream overwhelmed him.

"Pastor Gabriel told me about the shed and the glass case. You did good destroying it. It is an altar used to bring the beast power. With the release of the sixth demon, they will become flesh and evil will spread throughout the earth. Claire, you said you saw bones in a circle of stones. Where was this?" Father Taylor grabbed another book from his bag.

A dark shadow moved through the upstairs and Sara's door slowly opened. As the faceless figure moved next to Sara's bed, a voice whispered into the night, "Now." Its head turned towards the ceiling as its mouth dropped open and its whispers flooded the air as it put its hand across Sara's chest and she began to dream, as her bedroom door slammed shut.

. . .

SHE AWOKE *in her room looking around at her toys stacked neatly in her toy-box. She thought she could hear a voice in the distance calling her name amongst the howling sound of dogs, but she wasn't sure if it was her mother or someone else. As she crawled out of her bed and stepped out into the hallway, she noticed a light shining in, through the dark house, cascading across the wooden floor downstairs. "Mom," she called out, but no one answered. She walked down the stairs slowly, holding onto the rails, taking each step one at a time. The back door was open wide and the yard filled with an eerie fog as the wind howled through the trees as they swayed in the dark night. She stood staring out into the yard looking at the light by the pool shining through the back doorway. Dogs barked in the distance and she noticed a woman standing out near the field, under the willow tree. She felt as if she had seen her before. It frightened her but she wasn't sure why. The woman was beautiful with long black hair blowing in the wind and she called out to her, "Sara," holding out her hands. Sara stepped out the door and began to walk closer to the field. The sound of the woman's voice was hypnotic and Sara could feel herself being pulled closer towards her. "Sara," she called out to her again in an airy whispering voice. She could feel the wet grass beneath her bare feet and a chill ran through her from the cold air. As she reached the edge of the field, standing before the woman in the long flowing white dress, she was captivated by her hollow blue eyes that seemed to stare right through her. "Come," the woman said, taking Sara's hand and leading her farther into the field. The fog was so thick that all Sara could see was the grass blowing next to her and the woman walking with her, holding onto her hand just tight enough that she could feel the tips of her black nails poking just slightly into her skin. She wanted to pull away and run back into the house but something kept her walking out, farther into the field. The woman turned to Sara and looked down at her, her voice seemed to echo. "You must learn your true calling. Tonight, you will be marked for the future." She released Sara's hand and walked farther out in front of her before stopping in the distance and turning back to look at her again. Sara didn't understand what she was saying but she was frozen with fear and could no longer move her feet, which seemed to be locked firmly to the ground. The distance between them didn't lessen the intensity of the woman's frightening presence. Her cold blue eyes stared at Sara and her pale white skin shone through the moonlit night as her long black hair blew back in the wind. The woman looked up into the sky and raised her arms upward as she began to chant words that Sara could not understand. Sara could feel the ground rumble beneath her feet and out of the dirt rose five demons, three on one side and two on the other, standing between Sara and the woman forming a pathway between them. Sara tried to scream but when she opened her mouth, nothing came out. Her eyes opened wide with fear and she could feel her pulse racing through her as she tried to catch her breath, looking one by one at what had risen from the ground. The demons stood with rotten flesh that seem to hang down and drip off of their bodies. Their eyes big and black as the night with their faces distorted and their ears pointing up past the top of their heads. They stood staring through Sara as the woman stood at the end of the path and continued to chant. They opened their mouths and their sharp jagged teeth dripped a thick black mucous that ran down their lips as they looked up and let out screeching noises into the night air. Their arms elongated with long fingers and tarnished yellow nails and one of them looked at Sara and smiled an evil grin as it licked its lips hungrily at her standing frozen in the field. Sara's heart raced and tears flooded her eyes. She wanted to run but couldn't move her feet. Everything in her was screaming out at the top of her lungs but she couldn't make a sound. Her body began to tremble as the woman started to walk closer towards her. She could hear another sound above her and as she looked up, a flock of crows covered the night sky and flew above her, lingering in the air. 'Caw, caw, caw,' echoed all around her.*

. . .

CLAIRE HEARD the door slam upstairs, "Sara!" She ran up the stairs, but the door was locked shut. She could see a bright light coming from underneath the door and she screamed. Jason and the others were right behind her and Jason threw himself into the door to try and knock it open. "Sara!" he yelled. "Open the door!"

Father Taylor grabbed Claire's arm. "Quickly! Claire, where did you see the girl in the circle?" Claire ran to the attic while Jason continued to try and knock the door open. She turned and frantically searched the drawer for the hammer. Grabbing it, she rushed to the attic door and began to pull the nails out. "Jason, help me!" she screamed out.

He ran over, grabbed the hammer, and continued to remove all the nails from the door. They rushed in and Claire ran to the small door in the attic and flung it open. It was pitch black except a small light shining down in the corner. Claire looked in, "No!"

Father Taylor pushed her aside and looked into the room. Sara appeared to be lying in the circle surrounded by rocks with a strange glow about her.

"Sara!" screamed Claire as she struggled to reach her.

"It's not Sara! Quickly, hand me the book!" screamed Taylor.

Jason took hold of Claire, "It's not her! It's not her!"

Gabriel grabbed the book and handed it to Taylor who began to chant from the pages as he sprinkled the holy water into the small room towards Sara.

"Claire, Jason… give me your hands," Gabriel said looking at them and taking their hands, "God said: where two or more gathers in my name, I am with them. Tonight, we call on the name of God to be with us and give us strength. In the name of God! I command the morning to take hold of the ends of earth and shake the wicked out of it."

You could still hear Father Taylor chanting in the small room. "Saint Michael the Archangel, defend us in battle! Be our protection against the wickedness and snares of the devil!" He splashed the holy water onto what looked like Sara. The little girl's head turned around as her flesh became old and her eyes turned black and she spoke in a sound like rushing waters, "It's too late, it is done."

"I command you back to the pit of hell, in the name of The Father, The Son, and The Holy Ghost!" as he shouted, the girl's body turned to bones before his eyes.

As the woman reached Sara, she stretched out her arm and placed her hand on top of Sara's head. Her mouth dropped open and her jaw dislocated and she groaned fiercely looking up at the sky. Sara could feel her nails piercing through the top of her head as something cold and wet began to run down her forehead and her eyes rolled back into her head. Her entire body began to shake. She could hear nothing but the sound of the demons screaming out and the birds hovering above her in the field. She collapsed on the ground and everything faded to black.

* * *

Taylor looked back at Gabriel who was still praying holding onto Claire and Jason's hands. "Gabriel, get my bag. Hurry! And the shawl!"

Gabriel quickly ran down the stairs and grabbed the prayer shawl and Taylors black bag and returned to the attic. He handed it to Taylor.

Jason struggled with Sara's door, "It still won't open! Sara!" he yelled out.

Taylor reached into the room and grabbed the bones, wrapping them into the shawl before placing them into his bag. Just as he grabbed the last bone, the inside of the room changed again to nothing but insulation and Sara's door gave way to Jason as he fell into her bedroom.

"Sara!" Claire ran into the room and grabbed Sara who was still asleep, as if in a trance. Jason knelt beside her. "Wake up Sara! Wake up!"

Father Taylor and Gabriel stepped into her bedroom. "Claire, please!" Jason and Claire moved back and Taylor doused his fingers in holy water and marked the sign of the cross upon Sara's head and began to pray.

The back door swung open with a loud bang and Claire jerked her head towards the bedroom door. A gust of wind blew in from outside and Father Taylor yelled out. "The Lord will have dominion over the devil this night!" He put his hand on Sara's forehead. "In the name of the Lord, I bind you evil spirits and demons that occupy this house and send you to the foot of the cross to be judged by God! I bind any demons here and cast you out in the name of Lord! Oh, prince of the heavenly hosts, by the power of God, thrust into hell all the evil spirits and demons who prowl about in the night seeking this family!"

Sara tried to toss and turn but the priest steadied her. "Lord release this child from the prison that darkness holds over her!" Then he continued to pray in tongues.

Sara's body shook and her eyes rolled back into her head.

"RELEASE HER!" the priest yelled.

All at once everything stopped and Sara opened her eyes. The priest stepped back and Jason and Claire quickly lifted her up. "Mommy, what's going on? Who is that man?"

Claire let out a sigh of relief and hugged her tightly.

"It's okay," Jason said, stroking her hair. "This is Father Taylor; he is a friend of ours." He glanced back at the priest. "Thank you."

"Nice to meet you, Sara." With that Father Taylor grabbed his bag and him and Gabriel left the room smiling.

"It's okay, Sara. I'm not going to let anyone hurt you, ever. I promise you that," Claire said. She kissed the top of Sara's head and then picked her up. "You can sleep with us tonight."

"Dragonfly," Sara said, as she reached towards the shelf.

Claire picked up the dragonfly and handed it to her and took her downstairs to put her in bed with them for the night. Sara couldn't remember any of her dream but was exhausted and fell back asleep quickly.

The house grew calm and an immediate presence of peace washed over them. The priest looked at Jason and Gabriel. "Did you feel that? It's gone."

"Yes," Jason said, glancing back at Gabriel.

"The demon is gone," Gabriel said, giving him a comforting nod.

Claire could hear them talking but she didn't want to leave Sara and she curled up next to her in bed and held onto her tightly as she slept. "It's over," she thought.

Gabriel picked up their things as Father Taylor gripped the bag tightly in his hand, "I need to get these to the Vatican. I'll go tonight."

"We can't thank you enough," Jason said, shaking Gabriel's hand and then looking at Father Taylor again. "Thank you."

Father Taylor walked out the front door and stopped, turning around he looked at Jason, "You will always have to watch over her closely. The Hell Witch will no doubt try and gain access into your life again. The thing we destroyed in the attic. It was using it to open the door and channel its way in. That's gone, it will need another door to come through before it can reach you again. It has been stopped this time and when it tries to return it could become very dangerous to all of you. Just watch yourselves and everything that you bring in this house and around your daughter. It will be lurking in the shadows to try and find a way in. If you need me at any time in the future, please call me." He handed Jason a piece of paper with his phone number on it.

Jason looked at the piece of paper and back at Father Taylor. "No worries sir, we aren't going to do anything to let that thing back in here. I can promise you that."

Gabriel stopped and looked at Jason. "About your grandmother. I didn't know. I'm sorry. I wish she would have come to me for help." He shook his head. "Be mindful. Evil has its plan just like God does. Father Taylor is right, whatever you do, don't let that thing back in. They have a way of returning stronger than before."

Jason looked at him. "We will be in church on Sunday and nothing is getting back in this house."

As they got into their car and drove away, Jason thought he saw a dog across the street and jerked his head back towards the animal, but it was just a cat from down the road. He let out a sigh of relief and locked the house. "It's over," he said, as he plopped on the bed and pulled Claire close.

"Jason, I don't feel it here anymore." She cried as she hugged him. "It's really gone."

"It is, and tomorrow... I'm taking Sara fishing," Jason said. "You want to come?"

"No. You two have your time together. I have to finish up some work in the darkroom that is long overdue. I love you," she reached up and kissed him goodnight.

"I love you too," Jason said, and he held her until they fell asleep.

* * *

THE HALLS of the Vatican echoed with the footsteps of Father Taylor as he approached a small room with the Archbishops eagerly awaiting his arrival.

As he opened the door, their chatter turned to silence and they took a seat at the long wooden table.

Setting the bag down, he glanced at the men before locking eyes with the head Archbishop. "Your Excellency, I've found the source. I believe as long as the bones of the child are protected, she will be stopped."

The head Archbishop arose from his seat, took the bag, and blessed it with the sign of the cross. "You have done well Father." He opened a wooden chest and placed the bag of bones inside before nodding towards two of the other men at the table. "Please, take the chest and lock it in the Passetto di Borgo. It will be safe there." The two men picked up the chest and walked out the door.

Father Taylor bowed his head and gave the Archbishop a final glance before leaving the room, "Your Excellency." He took a deep breath as he walked back down the long hallway; however, he couldn't fight the eerie feeling that it wasn't over.

THE BEAR

*M*onths had passed since the night that Pastor Gabriel and Father Taylor had visited their home and ended the nights of terror in the house. They didn't talk about anything that had happened anymore. Some things were better left unspoken and more than anything, they wanted to move past it all. The days were quiet and the nightmares had gone, and every Sunday they were all in church like clockwork. Sara wouldn't go near the field anymore. She had no memory of anything that had occurred, but, the field frightened her, even though she didn't understand why. She would only run so close to it, before she would stop and stare out amongst the trees and then quickly turn back and run closer towards the house.

Jason fought his own fears. When it came to the pool, he couldn't bring himself to get in the water again. He would make up some excuse of wanting to cook or watch Claire and Sara swim or read a book on the deck, but Claire knew the truth. He was working himself up to it but wasn't quite there yet and she was never one to push him into anything. They all needed time in one way or another, and for her it was the attic that seemed to always haunt her thoughts. It was still nailed shut, and every now and then she would walk up the stairs with the hammer, ready to take the nails out of the door, but she always stopped just before doing it and stared at the door before walking back down the stairs and placing the hammer back into the drawer and closing it shut. At least peace had returned to their sleep and the demons had gone, but their lives would take a while longer to heal.

It was a Saturday afternoon when Claire and Jason decided to drive into town and take Sara to the park. The sun was shining bright and the trees were just the right shade of green, flowers were blooming everywhere and there wasn't a cloud in the sky. They drove into town, pulled into the park, and started to get out of the car when Jason noticed a Rottweiler sitting alone by the swings.

"Claire, do you see that dog over there by the swings?" he asked. He was surprised to see the dog and had hoped he would never see a dog like that again.

"Yeah, why? Do you think it bites?" Claire asked, as she opened her car door and stepped out of the car.

"I don't know," Jason answered, still staring at the dog. "Maybe we should go somewhere else."

"That's ridiculous, Jason," Claire said as she helped Sara out of the back seat. "It's not barking or anything. It actually looks pretty docile."

"Let's at least go to the swings on the other side. Just in case. I mean for Sara. We wouldn't want to go near it. What if it does bite? Better safe than sorry," he replied.

"I guess. I mean, if it's bothering you, we can just go across the street," Claire said, still a bit confused at Jason's sudden fear of dogs. She had forgotten all about the black dog from before.

They walked to the other side of the street, and Sara began going up and down the slide while Jason and Claire sat on the bench watching her. Every few minutes Jason couldn't help but glance back over his shoulder at the dog sitting by the big yellow swing set across the street on the other side of the park. After a while, Jason looked back again and the dog was nowhere in sight. He looked all around the park but he didn't see the dog anywhere. A part of him felt relief and he wondered if it was the same dog he had been seeing for months. Somewhere in the back of his mind, he expected to turn around and suddenly find the dog sitting next to him, with that same expressionless look on its face. Those dark eyes that seem to stare him down every time he found himself face to face with that particular dog. He took a deep breath and sat back on the bench and tried to put it out of his mind.

"Are you okay?" Claire asked, putting her hand on Jason's knee.

"Yes, it's nothing," he answered. He didn't want to bring up the dog and have to explain it to her. He wanted to put everything out of both of their minds. More than anything, he just wanted to get back to normal. They were finally happy again.

Claire sat on the bench watching Sara play on the swing set and she remembered her camera in the car.

"Oh Jason, my camera bag is in the car. I'm going to grab it and get some pictures of Sara playing." She got up and started to walk towards the car.

"Wait, you want me to get it?" Jason asked.

"No, I got it," she smiled, and continued to walk to the car.

Sara was playing on the big sky fort playground set. It was made of cedar, and had a three-story fort, with two big yellow tube slides that came down off the second and third story. Sara loved to climb up in the fort and pretend it was a huge doll's house. She had her new doll with her and was teaching her how to slide. As she reached the third story of the fort, she looked out the window and waved at Jason who was sitting on the bench below watching her.

"Hi Daddy!" she yelled down.

"Hi!" Jason yelled back up, smiling at her. "Be careful."

There was a flag pole that hung down off the third floor of the fort that had a big white flag which had the town's name sewn on it in big blue letters. Sara liked reaching outside the window and trying her best to touch it. As she leaned out almost able to touch the tip of it, a big black crow landed on the pole. Sara screamed and jumped back landing on the floor inside the fort. The bird didn't move but only sat there, seemingly unaffected by the high pitched scream that she had let out.

"Sara! Are you okay?" Jason yelled.

Sara didn't move but sat still on the floor of the fort, looking up through the window at the crow still perched on the pole.

"Sara?" Jason called, looking up at the fort and expecting her to look back out the window again.

The crow frightened Sara, and she was too scared to move or yell anything back to Jason.

Claire reached the car and grabbed the camera out of her bag. As she started to walk back over, she could see Jason crawling up into the Fort and she wondered what he was up to. She held her camera up and took a picture as she laughed a little under her breath.

Jason reached the top of the fort where Sara was sitting still on the floor looking out of the window at the black crow perched on the flag pole.

"Sara?" Jason bent down and pulled her towards him. "Are you okay? What's the matter?"

"I want to go Daddy, please," Sara said, looking at Jason. He looked out the window at the crow and back at her again. "Okay baby, let's go. How about I take you for ice cream in town?"

"Okay," Sara said, and that seem to put her mind at ease as they climbed back down the fort together.

Claire stood at the bottom, watching them climb out. "What's going on?"

"Ice cream," Jason said, dusting off his pants and giving Sara a wink. "We decided we want ice cream."

Claire looked confused at the two of them who looked like they were in some sort of conspiracy together. "Okay, I can go for ice cream. So, like now?"

"Yes," Sara said, and she glanced back one final time at the empty pole. The bird flew away. Demons have a way of leaving their mark on you even after they are gone.

They walked across the street and loaded back into the car and drove towards Main Street.

"Everything okay?" Claire asked Jason, glancing at him across the front seat.

"I think she got spooked by a bird," he said. "I don't know. I just wanted to get her out of there."

"I guess we all have our adjustments to make," Claire said. "We still don't know anything that she really went through."

"Let's just put it behind us and get ice cream. Everything has been fine for weeks. Let's not jinx ourselves by talking about it," he reached over and took Claire's hand.

They reached the big parking lot at the end of Main Street and parked the car. Claire noticed Pastor Gabriel standing outside of the church.

"Jason, why don't you go ahead and take Sara for ice cream. I don't really want any, and I want to say hi to Gabriel. He has done so much for us." She grabbed her camera from the front seat.

"Okay, come on Sara, looks like it's you and me," he smiled at Sara and took her hand as they started to walk towards the ice cream shop and Claire went the other direction towards the church.

"Gabriel!" Claire called out, as she stepped onto the grassy lawn of the church. "It's so good to see you." She smiled.

Gabriel walked over towards Claire and gave her a friendly hug, "Claire, how is one of my favorite people doing?"

"Good, really good," Claire said. "We haven't had anything

happen in the house and things are finally getting back to normal."

"That's great," Gabriel said. "Why don't you come in the church for a moment and get out of this heat so we can chat?"

"That sounds great," she said, and they walked inside the church and sat down in Gabriel's office. He was glad she stopped by because he wanted to talk to her about a new project for the church.

"We are redoing the church directory and I wondered if you might be interested in taking all the family photos. The church will pay you of course."

"Nonsense," Claire replied. "I would be happy to do it free of charge after everything you have done for us." They discussed the details while Jason and Sara hit the ice cream shop.

* * *

As they walked into the ice cream parlor, cookies and ice cream scents filled the air. Sara ran over to the big glass case holding all the different flavors of ice cream. She ran her finger over the glass, searching the different flavors until she settled on chocolate.

"Chocolate please!" she said excitedly looking up at Jason.

"One chocolate ice cream it is. Do you want it in a cup or the cone?" Jason asked looking down at her.

"The cone!" Sara said, and she ran over to one of the little tables by the front window and took a seat. "And a coke!"

"Okay," Jason said, and he ordered their ice cream and one coke before sitting down with it at the table.

As she started to eat her ice cream, she stared out the window, "Daddy, can no one ever get me anymore?"

Jason looked at her puzzled, "No baby, I'm not going to let anything happen to you. Why did you ask me that?"

She looked down at her ice cream cone, "I don't know... sometimes, I just get scared like something is going to hurt me."

Jason took Sara's hand. "Hey, I'm not going to let anyone hurt you, not ever. You understand? No one."

"Okay," Sara said. Just then, a tall woman approached their table and looked at her.

"I'm sorry," the woman said. "I couldn't help but recognize you. You're Jason Cole, right? Charlotte's grandson?"

Jason stood up from the table and put his hand out and shook her hand, "Yes, I am and this is my daughter, Sara. I'm sorry, have we met?"

"No," the woman said. "But I have been meaning to come by and introduce myself to you. I was a good friend of Charlotte's and actually your mother as well. I'm Kristina, I own the bookstore. I've met your wife Claire but I haven't seen her in a while, and I noticed you sitting in here and wanted to say hello and see if everything was alright. I'm very sorry about Charlotte."

"You're the woman that found her, right?" Jason asked.

"Yes, it was an awful tragedy," Kristina said. She looked over at Sara still consuming every drop of her ice cream as it tried to melt and run its way down her hand.

Jason glanced at Sara and pulled out a napkin, "Here, Sara." He laughed and looked back at Kristina, "Well it was nice meeting you. Claire is over at the church but she should be here shortly if you would like to join us?"

"Oh no, I don't want to impose on family day," Kristina said. "What a nice doll you have." She said looking at Sara who had her new doll sitting in a chair of its own.

"Thank you, her name is Krissy," Sara said smiling and licking the chocolate from her lips.

"You know, I have a friend that needs a new home," Kristina said as she reached in her bag and pulled out a small blue teddy bear with blue button eyes and handed it to Sara. "You think you can keep him for me?" she said with a smile.

"Oh, we couldn't," Jason said, looking at Kristina.

"Oh dad! I love him," Sara said, as she took the bear and placed it in the chair with her doll.

"Nonsense," Kristina said. "Charlotte and Cindy were like family to me. I would love for her to have it. Why, it's almost like they belong together."

"Thank you!" Sara said, still trying to finish her ice cream cone.

Jason looked at Kristina and smiled. "Thank you, it's been a rough start here but I think things are finally settling down."

"Wonderful, tell that wife of yours I said hello. I have to be going back to the shop. Sara enjoy your day. Jason, nice to finally meet you," and she shook Jason's hand and left the shop, walking back down the street to the bookstore.

Jason looked back towards the street but there was still no sign of Claire.

"Come on Sara, your mommy must be caught up at the church," Jason said as he cleaned her up and loaded her doll and new bear into her backpack.

They left the shop and as they were walking towards the parking lot, they noticed Claire coming out of the church. She looked happy and it wasn't often that Jason saw that look in her eyes anymore.

"Jason!" she said as she reached the car. "Pastor Gabriel just hired me to take family pictures for the new church directory. I'm so excited, finally work again." She laughed as she helped Sara in the backseat. "I mean, I'm not going to take any money from the church but it will be great working again."

Jason got in the car and looked at her, "That's great. I was wondering what was taking you so long. You missed ice cream."

"That's okay," Claire said. "I'm so happy everything is working out." She reached across the seat and kissed him.

They drove back home and this time when Jason reached the

bridge, he decided to go across. "Jason, you don't have to." Claire said.

"I do," Jason said. He drove across and this time he heard nothing.

They decided to take the day and go swimming which made Sara extra happy. It was a sunny afternoon and the breeze outside made for a perfect day and even Jason thought it was finally time to go into the water. If he could conquer his fear of the bridge, he could get past the water as well. They reached their house and pulled into the driveway and as soon as they got out of the car and opened the front door, Sara shot up the stairs to put on her swimsuit.

"Are you going swimming too?" Claire asked Jason curiously.

Jason grabbed her hand and pulled her to him, "I think so." He kissed her on the lips and they went into their bedroom to get dressed.

Sara shot down the stairs first with an arm full of toys. They walked out the door towards the pool and left everything they had been through to a distant memory.

Claire stopped and turned back, looking at the house, "Hang on a minute, I'll be right back."

"Okay," Jason said, and he continued towards the pool with Sara. She jumped in the shallow end.

Claire walked back into the house and went into the kitchen and opened the drawer and pulled out the hammer. She took a deep breath and walked up the stairs and as she approached the attic door, she felt that sick feeling in the bottom of her stomach, "No more," she said. With that she took the nails out of the door and then checked to make sure the knob was still locked. As she went back down the stairs and put the hammer back into the kitchen drawer, she felt a sense of control and relief. She walked back outside and got into the pool with Sara and looked up at Jason, "Come on." She smiled.

Jason ran and jumped into the water and for the first time he felt like he was home again.

"Where did you go," he asked Claire, as he wiped the water from his face.

"I just had something to do," she smiled and leaned over, kissing his cheek.

They swam all day until it was dark and then got out, dried off and went inside the house.

Jason looked at Claire, "How about you get Sara cleaned up and I'll throw on some gourmet hot dogs."

Claire laughed, "Okay, sounds great." She took Sara upstairs and got her ready for bed while Jason changed and went into the kitchen to make hot dogs.

As they started back down the stairs Sara turned around, "Oh I have to get something."

"Okay," Claire said, "Don't be long, you need to come down and eat."

"Okay," Sara said, running into her room and grabbing her backpack.

She pulled out her doll and placed it on her bed and then pulled out her new teddy bear and sat it next to her doll, "You live here now with us. This is your new home." Then she ran back downstairs to eat.

As they sat around the table eating hot dogs, they laughed about their day of playing in the pool.

"Mommy, can you read me a story tonight?" Sara asked as she looked at Claire.

Jason looked over and winked at Claire. "I thought I was reading you a story."

"I want Mommy to read it," Sara said, smiling.

"Okay," Claire said, "Looks like I win. Which story do you want me to read to you tonight?"

"A Tea Set for Frances!" she said excitedly, as she bounced in the chair.

Claire laughed, "Okay, I know just which book you're talking about it."

As they finished up Jason started to clean the kitchen, "Claire go ahead up. I'll clean up down here."

"Okay," Claire said, and she stood up and gave Jason a kiss. "Thank you. I love you."

"I love you too," he said, and then he reached down and gave Sara a hug. "And I love you too, munchkin."

Sara laughed as she hugged Jason back, "Love you too, Daddy. Goodnight!"

Claire followed Sara up to the bedroom and as Sara crawled into bed, she shoved her teddy bear and doll under the covers and moved over to make room for Claire.

Claire picked up the book and crawled into bed and began to read until Sara fell asleep. She laid in her bed holding Sara close to her, thinking of how peaceful the day had been. Soon she fell asleep as well.

The house was quiet and dark and Jason had just turned out the lights in their room and crawled into bed himself. He was laying there listening to the wind outside thinking about how good the day felt and how lucky he was to have Sara and Claire.

As Claire and Sara lay asleep in the bed, the teddy bear tucked firmly under Sara's arm and the attic door slowly creaked open.

As Jason drifted off to sleep, a thumping echoed from the bathroom like a fingernail hitting the countertop, making a familiar sound. Tap! Tap! Tap! Gasping, Jason's eyes shot wide open.

Made in the USA
Monee, IL
13 August 2023

40908680R00125